Take a Chance
& Other Stories of Starting Over

T. L. Cooper

The TLC Press

ISBN: 1-943736-03-0
ISBN-13: 978-1-943736-03-4

The TLC Press
PO Box 3243
Albany, Oregon 97321

Dedication

*These stories are dedicated to the people who started over with me every time
I took that chance on changing my life..*

Acknowledgments

I appreciate all the work Loay Abu-Husein put into creating the cover based on my vague description of what I wanted. I am also grateful for his ongoing love, support, and understanding as I pursue my creative endeavors.

Joanne Pence offered invaluable feedback on several of the short stories that made it into the book as well as those that didn't! I am grateful for her ongoing encouragement to get more of my work out into the public.

I am thankful to Teresa Appleton Lutz for offering her thoughts on earlier iterations of several of the short stories in this book.

I send my thanks to Dr. Julia Bouchard in Boise, Idaho for answering my questions in regards to an early version of Baby.

I am eternally grateful to the friends and family members who cheer me on when I'm lagging behind and feeling like completion is too far out of sight to find.

Table of Contents

Hello for Life

Tyla sank to the bench in front of the apartment building she'd just left. Unsure what to do, she pushed her hands into her strawberry blonde hair and pulled hard. She closed her eyes replaying her conversation with Devon in her thoughts. She opened her brown eyes and looked up through the white blooms on the ornamental pear tree shading the bench. The sky was so blue it reminded her of Van Gogh's *Church at Auvers*, or Brayden's eyes... *Why in the world does Dev think I should tell Brayden that I'm getting married? Does he know something I don't?*

She stood. *Forget it.* Devon was wrong. Telling Brayden couldn't possibly result in anything good. Either he'd try to talk her out of marrying Mason or he simply wouldn't care. She had no idea which reaction she preferred. Then again, maybe he'd just want one last night together, but she couldn't do that either. No, better to not risk it.

She turned a half step, looking down, and digging in her purse for her keys. Arms encircled her waist and her feet left the ground. "Ty, where the hell have you been? You just disappeared."

Brayden gently placed her down, and she stared up into his blue eyes. She loved his eyes. They sparkled like he knew the secret to life but wasn't about to share it. She opened her mouth, closed it, and fought the tears welling up in her eyes.

He stared into her eyes, and she felt like he could see right into her soul. He'd always unnerved her with his intensity. She looked away concentrating on an azalea in bloom near the apartment building. Words still failed her.

"Ty, it doesn't matter. You're here now. Why didn't you call after...."

"It's not like you called me." She looked him at him again. Anger flashed across her eyes beyond her control. *How dare he?* "And, just for the record, I did call. I left you a message. When you didn't call back, I took the hint." She swallowed. "I know. A new one for me."

"What message? What hint? I never got a message from you after that night."

"If you'd really wanted to contact me, you would've, so it really doesn't matter."

He ran a hand through his short dark hair and shook his head. "You're right. I could've called. I didn't think you wanted me to. You had all those damn rules." He swallowed.

She smiled. "I understand."

"So, did you come to see me, Ty?"

She sighed and shook her head slowly. She desperately wanted to answer the hope in his eyes with the answer he wanted. She looked up remembering how at five feet five, she'd always had to tiptoe to kiss him. The random thought that he must be at least six feet one crossed her mind.

"Let me guess. Devon?" The hardness in his voice surprised her.

"Yeah. I needed to tell him...."

"Of course, you always ran to him no matter what."

"He's my friend."

"Yeah, I know. I've heard it often enough."

"Where is this coming from? Are you serious?"

He clenched his jaw. "Ty, come on. You always shared more with him than me."

"He..."

"Don't say it again, please." He looked up at the sky. She followed his gaze. A fluffy, white cloud drifted by. It reminded her of an abstract heart. "I've heard it often enough."

She touched his arm. "We should talk."

He stared at her. "I'm not sure what there is to say. I never could compete with Devon."

"There was no competition."

2

He laughed. "Maybe not in your mind, but his presence was always there. You talked about him all the time."

"No, I…" She paused. Maybe she did. She looked down as she tried to control the quiver in her voice. "It wasn't like that."

After what felt like a long silence, she looked up.

He stared at her, his tone bitter. "He always knew more about you than you'd even let me glimpse, Tyla. He made it past your impenetrable wall. I never could. No matter how hard I tried."

"That's not true." Her voice trailed off; he wasn't completely wrong. She'd tried to let him in, but she'd never been able to get away from her fear that he'd use her vulnerabilities against her like so many other guys had. She'd never given him a fair chance. She looked at him as she searched for the right words. She'd walked away so he could find someone who could be the woman he needed, deserved, the woman she could never be. "Okay, maybe you have a point, but it wasn't because I didn't care."

"Ty, I never doubted you cared, but you didn't trust me. Without trust we were stuck."

"I wanted to trust you if that makes any difference." She had always trusted him. Still did. But… She never trusted herself enough to trust her own judgment. She looked past him, avoiding his eyes. *I should walk away. Let him hate me.*

He stared at her for a long time. "What did I…" He looked up at the tree.

"Oh, Bray, you didn't do anything to deserve the way I treated you. You didn't do anything wrong." She took his hand without thinking surprised by how right, how natural, it felt. "I was a mess. Trust scared me. Kindness scared me. Good scared me. Your honesty scared me. Imagining a future with you terrified me and yet I couldn't stop myself. Imagining a future in which you left me also terrified me, yet I was sure it would happen when you really got to know me." She fought back tears.

"Tyla, I loved you. I still do."

Her tears broke through. He'd never professed love before. Her heart pounded in her chest. She heard words coming from her mouth that she didn't recognize nor could she stop. "I love you, too, Bray."

She stared at him a long moment without moving, hyperaware of every inhalation and exhalation they each took. He squeezed her hand, his expression pained. "What's this?"

Before she could respond he lifted her hand. "*A diamond ring.*" He swallowed hard. "*An engagement ring.* You profess... you say... and you..." He dropped her hand. "I thought you never wanted to... You said..." He turned and walked away.

"Wait, Brayden, please." He stopped without turning back, his body rigid. "Please, don't walk away."

He turned. Anger flashed in his eyes, but she thought he also blinked back a tear, or maybe she saw what she wanted to see. "Ty, I can't do this. I just can't." He shook his head. "Just tell me one thing. Were you dating him at the same time we...."

"No. Of course not. How could you even think that?"

"Uh. How about your insistence we not call our relationship a relationship."

She sighed. "But that didn't mean I... Okay, that sounds lame even to me. But I thought you knew how I..."

"Ty, you disappeared. I had no idea why or where you went. Now you show up engaged." He grabbed her hand with the ring again. "What am I supposed to do with this?"

"I know how it looks." She swallowed hard. "Can we get a cup of coffee or something? I want to explain."

He looked at his watch. "Ty... I...Fine. Give me twenty minutes." He turned toward the apartment building. She sat down on the bench. He looked over his shoulder. "Are you coming in or what?"

"Are you sure?"

He laughed. "I'm not going to seduce you. I need to feed Hope and put my laptop inside."

"I wasn't worried about that." She mumbled under her breath though her heart pounded at the idea. A part of her wished he would.

He opened the front door of his apartment and a ten-month-old brown and black German Shepherd with huge brown eyes greeted them with a tail wagging so fast it was blur. Brayden petted her. "When did you get a dog?"

"I brought her to you at your apartment, but your landlord told me you'd moved out the day before, so I brought her home with me." He scratched Hope behind the ear. He walked toward the kitchen with Hope by his side. "Ready for food, Hope?"

Tyla watched the interaction and smiled. Hope moved away from Brayden and walked over to her. She placed her head on Tyla's thigh. Tyla petted her head and neck. "She's beautiful. What do you mean you brought her to me?"

"I was volunteering at the shelter when she was brought in with her mom and two siblings. She reminded me of you. It was something in her eyes. I kept going back to the kennel and every time she would run over and sit at the door looking up at me. So much sadness, strength, and hope in her attitude." He shrugged. "So I adopted her for you."

Tyla fought back the tears that welled up in the corners of her eyes. "Sounds like she adopted you." She leaned down close to Hope's ear and whispered. "Smart girl."

"I know it's usually not a good idea to give pets as presents, but I know how badly you want – wanted – a dog."

"Still do." She nuzzled Hope's nose. "I love dogs."

They sat in silence for a minute. "Wait a minute. I didn't know you volunteered at the shelter."

"Oh, it wasn't a regular thing. It never really came up. I volunteered sometimes during the summer and once in a while when they were shorthanded during the school year. They called and asked me last minute. You were so busy, we hadn't really talked. I realized later you were avoiding me."

"No, I wasn't. I…" The look in his eyes stopped her comment.

Hope left Tyla as Brayden placed a stainless steel food bowl in its raised stand. She started eating. Brayden joined Tyla at the table.

"Brayden, really, I wasn't avoiding you. I just didn't know what was going on with me. I needed to figure some things out. And, when you didn't call…"

"Figure out some things about us?"

"About my life. And since that included you, I guess about us as well."

"Why didn't you talk to me?"

"I felt like you'd be better off without me. I'd been making you miserable for quite a while, and we both know it. Besides, after I left you that message…"

"First, that's my decision. And, second, I wasn't miserable when we were together. The only thing that made me miserable was when you left." He looked out the window while she squirmed. "You're determined to discuss that message, aren't you?"

"Not really. It's just that it changed things."

"What did you say?"

"Basically, I said I really enjoyed that night, and if you wanted to get together again to give me a call. If you didn't, I'd understand."

"I never called, so you assumed."

She nodded.

"Damn it, Tyla." He sighed. "And you gave up just like that. One phone call. Poof."

"I didn't want to get all stalkerish on you."

"That's just so you, Ty."

She shrugged. "Why didn't you call?"

"I didn't get the message. Dirk likely deleted it."

She nodded. "I can see him doing that. He never liked me."

"I never cared what he thought."

"So you would've called?" She swallowed. "If you'd gotten the message?"

"Duh, I adopted a dog for you, Ty, even if you were no longer there by then."

She wiped at the tears spilling down her cheeks but didn't speak.

After a moment of uncomfortable silence, he sighed and ran his head over his head. "Tyla, it hasn't even been six months. How can you already be engaged?"

She closed her eyes. "It's a long story."

"I've got all day."

She smiled and looked deep into his bright blue eyes. They sparkled now not with his usual humor but with frustration, annoyance, hurt, and anger. "You were always too good to me. I never could quite trust that."

"Do you have any idea how ridiculous that sounds?"

She stared at him. She listened to Hope greedily lap the water from her water bowl. She listened for the sound of a ticking clock, but there wasn't one. She looked past Brayden's head to a potted plant in the corner. the Chinese Evergreen she bought him months ago because she wanted to give him something that brought life to his home and filtered the air at the same time. She heard her own heart beat and was certain it faltered. A tear slipped down her cheek. She couldn't believe she kept crying. She really wasn't a crier. "Yes, actually, I do. But it also makes perfect sense."

"In what universe does not trusting someone who is good to you make sense? In what world do you leave someone who thinks you're the most wonderful woman in the world without a word – not one, single world?"

Hope dropped her leash in Brayden's lap. He attached it to her collar while Tyla sat there unsure how to respond. She watched her thumbs as she flicked her thumbnails against one another. He stood. "Let's walk over to Jumpin' Java. They allow dogs. We can get a cup of coffee and talk. Besides Hope needs her walk."

She nodded still unable to speak. If she opened her mouth, she'd sob. A tear slipping down her face was one thing, but out-and-out sobs were unacceptable. She followed him out the door still trying to get control of her emotions.

Brayden turned them to walk through the park. The park offered a little oasis in the middle of way too much concrete. Green grass, a mix of evergreens and deciduous trees and plants, a well worn dirt path, and discreet picnic areas made for a lovely walk. They couldn't see the playground area from the path he chose, but the sounds of children playing and laughing easily reached them. Hope sniffed, walked proudly, looked around the area, and wagged her tail. Tyla loved the way she looked up to Brayden for direction, and the way he answered her often with only a sound or a nod. "Tyla, this is the longest I've ever seen you not speak."

"Bray, I don't know what to say. I have no answer for your questions. The only thing I've got is what I've already said. I thought it would be better for you if I was out of your life."

He inhaled deeply and let the breath creep out. They walked on in silence. Tyla feared the next sentence would be the one that changed everything forever, but then she feared it every time one of them spoke. All the most important things they needed to say begged to be spoken. Everything she'd ever feared him seeing in her fought her attempts to keep them hidden. Maybe they'd never been as hidden as she thought...

Once they were seated at an outdoor table at Jumpin' Java, he picked up her hand with his right hand and pointed at the ring with his left index finger. "Okay, tell me about this. Who is he? Do you love him? Is this what you really want?"

She looked up at him, sipped her coffee, and said, "Fine. Here goes. I met him about a month after I left here. An old friend introduced us. We had some interesting conversations." She shrugged. "Seeing you is making me doubt my feelings for him if you want the truth, but I thought I loved him. And, when I said yes, it felt right. Now...." She looked toward the street. She watched a few cars pass. "What about you, Bray? Are you dating anyone?"

He didn't answer until she turned and looked at his face. "Not exclusively. I date, but I'm not in a relationship." He took a sip of coffee. "I have to ask. Are you pregnant?"

She laughed. "No, I'm not. Everyone asks that same question. I wondered when you were going to get there."

He shrugged. "Of course they do. This all seems very sudden."

"I know." She paused. "Why is it that trying to explain it to you makes it seems so ridiculous when I was so sure of everything before?"

"Maybe because you know I won't believe your rationalizations."

"Maybe."

"You owe me more than you thought leaving would be best for me. That isn't a reason."

"You're right. I owe you an explanation, but none of the reasons I had make sense now. Looking into your eyes all I want is to..." She closed her eyes against the tears that threatened once more. When she opened her eyes, she couldn't read his expression, but the hurt in his eyes made her heart ache. She choked back a sob.

He leaned forward. "Is to what, Ty?"

She sighed. "I've never been good at being vulnerable. You know that. Talking about this makes me feel vulnerable."

He nodded but stayed silent, waiting.

"Okay, fine," she said. "All I want to do is beg your forgiveness and ask you to give me another chance. I look at this ring on my finger, and I want to rip it off. I'm questioning everything I thought was true. I feel like no matter what decision I make it's going to be the wrong one. On top of that, I can't seem to stop these damn waterworks..."

"Tyla, as much as I want to, I can't give you another chance without knowing what the hell happened." He reached across the table and took her hand in his. "You always kept me at arm's length, but you don't have any problem letting this guy in. I mean, you're already marrying him."

"I…" She swallowed hard. A realization hit her like a brick. She took a deep breath. She had to tell him the truth. If he didn't understand, at least it would be out there. "Because I'm an idiot. Because you're exactly what I want and what I need. I can't handle that. He keeps me guessing. And, honestly, if he walked away tomorrow, I'd be okay. If you did, I'm afraid I'd never get over it."

"Again, Ty, that's ludicrous. People marry people they want to spend their lives with not people they can let walk away easily."

"Which is exactly why you're better off without me! You need a woman who isn't so scarred that your goodness, your honesty, your understanding terrifies her, who can not only love you but express that love without fear."

"I never asked any of that from you. Never. I've never asked you to be anything other than who you are."

"I know, but you see something in me that doesn't exist."

"That's not true."

"No, I'm right. You see what you wish I was. I can't live up to that image."

"You're too hard on yourself. You always have been. You blind yourself to the good in you because if you don't admit it's there, you can give everyone else an excuse for mistreating you. I've watched you do it too many times, even with Devon."

"What do you want from me?" Tears streamed down her cheeks. Her nose started to run, and she felt her cheeks turn red. Her heart pounded. The terror of the moment held her in its grip and refused to release her.

He sighed, tapped his fingers on the table, and looked away. His next words sliced through her heart. "You."

She twisted the diamond ring around her finger and stared at it. She pulled it off and put it back on. She looked into Brayden's eyes and asked, her voiced barely above a whisper. "But what if I let down my guard and you hate the person you see?"

"That's always been the problem, hasn't it? What is it you think I'll hate so much? That you're not perfect? I've never thought you were perfect. I never wanted you to be perfect. I'm sure as hell not."

She stared at the coffee swirling in her cup as she gently turned the cup. "But I'm damaged goods."

Anger flashed across his face. "Don't you ever say that again. You are not damaged goods. You're a survivor. You're resilient. You are one of the strongest people I know."

"So are you saying you'd be willing to give me another chance?"

When Brayden didn't answer, Tyla looked up. He stared at her. Hope moved over to lick Tyla's arm. Tyla petted her while waiting for Brayden to answer. Finally, he sighed. "What about that?" He pointed at her finger again.

She slipped the ring from her finger and stared at it. "I can't do this if I have these questions, these doubts, these feelings. How do I explain this? I don't want to hurt him. He doesn't deserve that."

"Tyla, I don't know, but honesty is generally the best bet. Isn't it better to hurt him now than to get even more immersed and hurt him more later?" He squeezed her hand. "You do honesty well as I recall."

"Except when I run away." A smile tugged at the corners of her mouth.

He didn't smile, not even a little bit. He ran his finger around the top of his coffee cup as he clenched and unclenched his jaw.

"I don't know if I'd be doing this because of me or because of you," she said.

"That's a question you have to answer for yourself." He paused. "However, you have to know I'm not letting you walk away so easily this time."

She held her breath and squeaked. "What do you mean?"

"What do you think I mean?"

The look in his silenced her. She wasn't sure what she wanted him to say.

He sighed. "Oh, Ty, come on. When you dropped me off at work that last morning I saw you, you said goodbye and you never say goodbye – ever. I knew something was up. I should've said something. I don't know what, but something."

Tyla twisted the ring around in her fingers and stared at it.

"What could I have said, Ty? I mean really. Was there anything?"

"Stay."

"Excuse me."

She looked into his eyes. "If you had said "stay", that's all it would've taken."

He laughed. "Are you serious?

"What?"

"You really want me to believe that's all it would've taken? Seriously? Come on."

"If just once you'd looked at me and said enough of this crap. Either we're together or we're not. Enough of these damned rules. Let's take a chance and just be together. If you'd just said that to me..."

"You would've run for the hills."

"No, I wouldn't have. I fantasized all the time about exactly that. About you saying those words to me, so I could finally tell you the truth about how I felt, about what I wanted us to be."

"I don't believe you. Every time I even came close, you changed the subject or you ran away. You never let the conversation go there. Never. And you know it."

Her cheeks turned a deep pink. "I...I...I really did fantasize about it."

They sat in silence. Tyla looked around the sidewalk seating area of the coffee shop while Brayden stared at traffic. Neither quite knew where to take the conversation from there. They could only rehash the past for so long...

Brayden stood and stretched. "I need another cup of coffee. How about you?"

"Sure. And, maybe a blueberry scone?" She lifted her purse. "Let me."

"I've got it."

While he was gone, she tried to figure out what to do next. Brayden was a wonderful man, and he deserved to be happy. She just didn't think he could be happy, truly happy, if he was with her. He seemed so innocent to her, and she was anything but innocent. She watched him stand at the counter waiting for their order. Suddenly she felt the desire to grab her purse and run as fast as she could. Hope licked her hand. She looked into the dog's eyes and knew she would sit right there and wait to see what happened.

"I about half expected you to be gone when I got back."

Brayden's voice cut through her thoughts.

"You got me a dog and kept her."

"What?"

"Nothing. Just a thought I had while you were inside."

"Maybe you should share."

"Maybe, but I'm not sure it would make sense to you."

"Try me."

"I'm not sure it makes sense to me." She smiled and took a bite of scone.

"Ah, now why doesn't that surprise me?"

She laughed. "Because you've heard it a dozen times."

"At least."

"And, I was always right."

"No, you weren't. Sometimes I helped you understand things better."

She felt silence settle between them but did nothing to stop it.

"Didn't I? I always thought I did."

"You always tried, Bray. And, I loved you for that. It's just there are some experiences that your life experience will never equip you to understand. You can't help that."

"And, this fiancé is better equipped to understand?"

"No, but he doesn't try to fix me." The words were out before she could stop them.

"Damn it…"

"Wait, you don't understand. Wait. Please hear me out. That didn't come out right." She placed a hand on his forearm. "Really. This one I can explain."

"Fine. Explain. Quickly."

"I'm not saying you were trying to fix me. I know you loved me for who I am, but I felt broken. I was trying to fix myself, and you did everything you could to help me. Sometimes you tried too hard."

"Are you fucking kidding me? I tried too hard." He clenched his jaw. "You have got to be the only woman in the world who faults a guy for actually trying."

She swallowed hard. "He doesn't do anything. He's just there. He's not supportive. He doesn't ask. He doesn't want to hear about it. He leaves me to figure things out on my own."

"Sounds like he either doesn't care or he doesn't want to face the reality of your situation. Or maybe it's worse than that. Maybe he doesn't believe you."

That hadn't occurred to her. "I don't think that's it. I think he just realizes this is something I have to resolve on my own. I have to find a way to make peace with it and move on. He's all about the moving on – moving forward – leaving the past in the past."

"If only life were that simple." Brayden raised an eyebrow.

"For him it is."

"Really? Or is that just what he says when you want to talk about you?"

She stared out at traffic. Brayden had a way of getting to her, of making her think. She hated that sometimes.

"Tyla, I don't know where we go from here. I just know I want you in my life. I don't even know if that's possible."

"I don't know, Brayden. I really don't. But, I know I can't get married if seeing you causes this reaction." A tear slipped down her cheek. "I'm afraid of what this means. I'm afraid of what happens no matter what I do. No matter what I do right now, someone gets hurt. Maybe we all get hurt."

"But what do you want? Isn't that the real question?"

"Is it, Bray? There are three people involved here. I think what each of us wants matters."

"Yes, but you shouldn't do anything you don't want to do. Ever!"

"None of us should."

"Tyla, damn it, you're avoiding the question. Right this moment, what do you want to do?"

"I'm not answering that." She felt her cheeks redden as she blushed.

She watched as the message behind her words hit their mark. "Oh… Well, Tyla, even if we were back together that would have to wait. We'd have to…"

"I know that, but you asked what I wanted."

"And, hell yes, I want the same thing. It's taken every ounce of self-restraint I have to not touch you, to not hold you, to not…"

"Okay, I think we'd better leave this here."

"Probably." He looked at his hands. "What now?"

"I really don't know, but I don't want to walk away from you. I can't imagine never speaking to you again. I can't imagine never..." She swallowed hard. "I need to think. I need to talk to him. I need..." She wiped a tear away. "*you*."

He stood. "We can't change things in the course of a single conversation. You're right about one thing. You need to know what you want. But I need to think, too. I'm not sure how we recover from this."

She nodded but didn't stand. "I know. I don't deserve another chance with you. And, asking you to give me time to figure this out isn't fair. Neither is just walking away from him."

"But it was fair to just walk away from me?" His voice turned hard.

"No, that's not what I meant at all." She looked up. "Bray, what I did to you was unforgiveable."

"No, not unforgiveable but it was unforgettable. If it was unforgiveable, I wouldn't even be talking to you." He picked up Hope's leash. "Look, I've got to get home. I've got a ton of stuff to do before class tomorrow."

"Okay." She still didn't stand.

"Ty, come on."

"What? I thought you were saying goodbye."

"Don't be ridiculous. I'll walk you back to your car."

"You don't have to."

He sighed. "I know I don't have to. Ty, I'm not saying I don't want to try, but I am saying I can't wait forever for you to decide. I love you. That hasn't changed, but if you're going to marry someone else..."

"I know."

They walked back toward his apartment in silence and veered into the parking lot when they arrived. At her car, he reached up and wiped the tears from her eyes. She looked up at him. He leaned down and kissed her gently. She kissed him back and felt the passion build between them. After a moment, they broke away. They looked into each other eyes for a long moment before turning away. She leaned against the car remembering...

She shook her head, but that didn't stop the wobbly feeling in her knees. His kisses never failed to elicit that response from her. Every time it happened she reminded herself that only happened in fiction, but her knees belied her conviction. She looked at him again. Then reached into her purse and pulled out a small notebook. She scribbled her phone number and her address on it, ripped the page from the notebook, and handed it to him. "Call me if you want. If you don't, I'll understand."

He took the paper, folded it, and clutched it in his hand. "I will, but I hope you'll call before I get the chance."

She nodded unable to find words.

He turned to leave. She mumbled, "Brayden, I love you. I really do."

His voice was sad when he replied "Stay."

She sat in her car and watched him talk to Hope as he walked away. He glanced back over his shoulder, and she started to cry again. She started the car as he rounded the corner out of her line of sight. She gasped for air to fill her empty lungs. Then she struggled to exhale. *Is this what it feels like to suffocate?* She turned the car off. She whispered his parting word to the empty car "Stay." *Was it enough?*

She opened the car door, stepped out, took a deep breath, and ran all the way to his front door.

She pounded on his door with both fists like she was trying to break it down. He opened the door, and she flung herself into his arms. Without a word, she closed the door behind them and kissed him. She kissed him with every ounce of passion in her body. She kissed him until he gently pushed her back. He opened his mouth to speak. She put her finger to his lips and whispered "Stay." Then she kissed him again.

She tore at his clothes. Her desire to feel his touch, her need to bask in his embrace, her need to feel him intimately overwhelmed her. Her love for him, her passion for him, her need to give him everything he deserved took control. She no longer wanted to fight it. She loved him. She knew it. He knew it. Fighting their desire, their love, made no sense. He gently held her away and looked into her eyes before meeting her every passionate move with his own.

The next morning she smoothed his hair and slipped quietly from the bed. She traced the little smile on his face gently enough to not wake him. He always seemed so innocent to her, so everything she wasn't. She hadn't wanted to ruin him, so she'd left. She hadn't wanted her own ruination to taint his life, so she'd pushed him away. She'd wanted what was best for him, and she'd been so sure that wasn't her. Somehow she'd forgotten that he had a say in those matters.

She placed the note she'd written on his pillow and slipped out of the house careful to not make a sound. She wanted him to read the note after she was gone, so he couldn't stop her from leaving. She knew what she had to do and she knew if he awoke he'd convince her to stay. She needed to get this over with, so she could move on.

As she drove she imagined him waking, realizing she was gone, and then seeing the note on the pillow where her head should have been. He frowned and opened the note.

Dear Bray,

Regardless of what you might be thinking right now,
I'm not sorry about last night. I hope you're not either.
I know now what I have to do. I hope you will
understand why I left. I called Mason, and I'm meeting
him for breakfast. I'm giving his ring back.
There's no question in my mind that I belong with you
if you want to try us again. I understand if you need to
think about this because I don't want what we had. I
want something better. I want something more real
than what we ever had.
We had romance. We had infatuation.
I want real love with you. I want lasting love with you.
I want you in my life for the duration. I want us to find
a way when things get difficult. I want to tell you all
my secrets and to hear all yours. I want to comfort
your pains and celebrate your successes. I want us to
grow together. I want us to laugh together, to cry
together, to figure out life together.
I realize that might not be what you want, but if it is,
be at my house tonight at six. We'll take it from there.
I urge you to think about it though and only come if
you really want to pursue a real, lasting love with all
the work that entails and all the joy that brings.

No matter what you decide, know that I will love you for the rest of my life and I will always be here if you need me.
I hope I see you tonight!
Love,
Ty

When the doorbell rang Tyla looked up from the cucumber she was chopping for a salad and glanced at the clock. It was only 5:15. Her heart pounded as she walked to the front door. She opened the door to find Brayden standing there with Hope. "Hi, Tyla, sorry I'm early."

She hugged him without speaking. "I'm not. I'm not sorry at all. I'm just so glad you came." She buried her head in his chest with a deep sigh and a huge smile.

"What's with the deep sigh?"

"I'm just so relieved you're here. I was so afraid you wouldn't show up. I was terrified last night was goodbye for you when it was hello for me."

He laughed. "Hello? Actually, I was thinking it was I love you and I'm never letting you go, so hello doesn't quite cut it."

She laughed and wiped away her tears. "Then let's go figure out how to make it hello for life."

Untraditional

Yasmin watched Nathan drop to his knee and knew what was coming. He pulled the red ring box from his pocket as she closed her eyes and whispered, almost inaudibly. "Please don't. Please."

She opened her eyes as he opened the box. She stared at the ring thinking about how many meals the money he spent on that stupid ring could buy for people in need. She sighed and looked down into his hopeful, joy-filled brown eyes. He'd always been the romantic one. She'd always been the one who wasn't quite convinced traditional norms meant anything. *Had he not listened?* All those times she'd told him her opinion on marriage and weddings and even relationships. Apparently not.

She looked down at him and hated to disappoint him, but she couldn't accept. She couldn't betray her stance. She couldn't betray herself. She loved him, but this wasn't what she wanted. *Why hadn't he left well enough alone?*

The ridiculous emerald cut diamond sparkled as the candles around them flickered. She turned her gaze to the two white and red roses in the vase on the table. She looked at the immaculate white tablecloth, red linen napkins, champagne glasses with the bubbles still rising in the quarter of a glass left, and the empty plates that had held their overpriced desserts following their overpriced meal. The whole evening should have been a clue. His nervous demeanor from the moment he picked her up and his casual flattery all evening suddenly made sense. She closed her blue eyes.

"Yasmin, will you…"

She lifted a hand and spoke softly, "Nate." She reached over and placed her hand on his closely shaven face. "I love you, but please don't do this."

She watched his apprehension build matching her own before he said, "But, I thought you wanted us to spend the rest of our lives together."

She sighed, "Please sit back down and let's talk."

He stood to his full six foot height and she couldn't help but admire his runner's frame and short dark hair. As he sat back down, she looked over at him and sighed. "Nate, honey, I'm not sure we need to equate the rest of our lives with marriage."

"That's the next logical step."

"No, that's the next traditional step."

This time he sighed. "Semantics."

"No, it's not. It's an important distinction because there can be many logical steps from where we're at. That's up to us to decide. We don't have to follow the traditions just because that's what other people have done."

"You've said that so many times."

"Yes, I have, so I'm more than a little surprised you decided to propose."

"But you supported and fought for gay people to have the right to get married."

"So?"

"If you hate marriage so much, why would you do that?"

She ran a hand through her auburn hair and sighed. "Because that's about equality. That's about civil rights. That's about people being treated fairly. It's not about my personal decisions. All people should have the right to make that decision for themselves."

"I thought you just never thought I'd ask."

She raised an eyebrow at him and stifled a laugh. "Seriously? I know you, Nate. You're a romantic. You love tradition. I tried to make my stance clear to you, so we wouldn't end up here."

"I still don't understand your objection. Our marriage will be ours not what others say it should be."

She sighed. "It's the institution itself that I object to. The whole idea is outdated and ridiculous. The ceremony is an ancient transfer of property, and I am no one's property."

"I never said you were. I've never treated you like property."

"I didn't say you had. I'm simply pointing out my problems with the institution. It's another way to keep women in their place."

"But ours wouldn't be."

"Maybe not, but that's not the point. I don't want to be married." She looked around the room at all the couple. "I don't want to be anyone's wife."

"We could just do a really long engagement." He glanced toward the ring.

"I don't want to be engaged either." A spark of anger bled into her voice. "What in the world made you think I'd want a diamond ring? Given my feelings about the diamond industry's mistreatment of miners and manipulation of the market, I just can't understand what made you think buying me a diamond was a good idea."

"It's romantic. It's the gesture."

"It's manipulation based on an advertising campaign." She looked at the ring. "I hope you can return it because even if I was willing to get married, I wouldn't want it."

Her heart ached at the crestfallen look on his face. "Nate, *if* I was willing to marry anyone, it would be you. This isn't about whether or not I love you. It's about who I am and the values I live my life by. I understand you have this dream of being a traditional family with a traditional marriage. I just can't give that to you, so if that's what you want, I love you enough to let you go find it. But, I have to be true to my values because if I'm not I'll grow to resent us both. And, that'll just make us both miserable."

He looked toward the window. She followed his gaze with her own. They both watched the traffic inch by as the traffic light turned from red to green. After a few minutes he turned back to her. "Yas, it's not like that. I love you, and I want to spend the rest of my life with you. It's not so much about getting married as it is about making us making that commitment."

She nodded and said quietly, "When we first started dating, you told me you couldn't imagine being with only one woman for the rest of your life. Now you're talking commitment..."

"Is that why you don't want to get married?"

"No. That has nothing to do with it. Remember you told me that after the first time I told you I never wanted to get married."

"Fair enough." He smiled. "But now I can't imagine being with anyone but you."

She smiled and said. "Commitment doesn't have to mean that. I don't ever want you to feel trapped."

He closed the lid on the ring box and picked up his champagne glass pointing it slightly toward hers. She picked up her glass and held it up. He said, "Here's to being untraditional…"

Letting the Dream Go

Willa attempted to shake off the previous night's dream. She needed to let it go but wasn't sure she possessed the desire. Willa needed the pain as palpable as it felt. It was all she had left. Awaking hurt. Her heart thumped against her breastbone. Her lungs struggled to release the carbon dioxide inside.

Willa looked in the mirror and squeezed her red-rimmed green eyes against the reality of the day. In her dream, Derrick held her. He stroked her hair. He wiped away her tears. His love fully enveloped her. He promised forever. She believed him.

Reality forced her eyes open as she sank onto the bed. The emptiness of the bed mirrored the hole he'd left in her life – in her soul. She rubbed her hand down the slight indention still in the sheets. He'd slept there only days before. Her dreams then had been of them building a future together. Dreams she'd taken for granted. Dreams she hadn't appreciated or fully grasped.

Images bombarded her. He smiled at her as only he could with that one crooked eye tooth on the left side. He'd always said it gave him character. Looking into his mud colored eyes felt like sinking into warm, sweet quicksand. She reached out to smooth his slightly ruffled light brown hair. Her hand moved through it like he was a projection. She jerked her arm back. Time to go. She checked her makeup in the mirror one last time. She looked presentable. Presentable was the best she could do.

Willa gulped hard and blinked her dry eyes. Tears didn't fall. There weren't any left to fall. Apparently, the possibility to cry her eyes dry actually existed.

She turned her concentration to driving. She needed to focus on one task at a time in order to survive the day.

Words swirled around her as she sat in a room filled with people. They sounded so far away. They were supposed to make her feel better, but they didn't. Only immersion in her dream made her feel better. She closed her eyes seeing his face just like she had the night before in the dream. She wanted that dream, needed that dream. Its images floated just out of reach. In that dream he hadn't deserted her. The words continued. She wondered what all these people said.

She tried to focus on her surroundings, but she really just wanted to drown in her dream. She let out a slow even breath. The pain in her chest squeezed the grief into a tight ball. The words hardened the knot.

What did any of these people know? They hadn't lain next to his even breath and warm, strong body night after night. They didn't face a future missing his embrace. They didn't wake up with their nose next to his pillow inhaling his fading scent or strive to protect the indention his body last left on the bed. They wouldn't be afraid if they changed the sheets, they would never smell the scent that was his alone. They didn't fear letting go would mean he would stop appearing in their dreams. No, that pain was reserved for her and her alone.

A hand touched Willa's shoulder. She shifted in her chair. *Why must they pull me from the dream over and over?* She smiled "Thank you." *Why did I thank this woman? Who is she?* The woman moved on.

She closed her eyes again and reached for the dream. She wanted to hold on to the vision of his smiling face. She longed to sleep and dream forever.

A hand touched hers. She looked up at a man who said more words that sounded a lot like all the other words she'd heard that day. His wasn't the voice she yearned to hear – the voice she'd never hear again.

All she wanted to do was bring her dream to life. Then there would be no reason to be here. She rubbed her hand on the emerald dress he'd wanted her to wear today so her "green eyes would shine," reached up to wrap an errant strand of hair behind her ear, and looked forward.

Someone lead her toward the front of the room. In her dream, she wore this dress. He wore his best suit, gray with an abstract patterned green and blue tie. They danced. He whispered "Happy Anniversary, My Love" against her ear. It tickled. She giggled. She kissed his cheek, then his lips. They laughed. They loved. They lived.

She leaned forward. There he lay motionless, eyes closed, wearing that same suit. She placed her head next to his ear and whispered in his unhearing ear. "Happy Anniversary, My Love."

Her dream ended.

Baby

Aerial settled behind the steering wheel and hesitated before turning the key in the ignition. She still couldn't quite believe the doctor's words. Her eyes hurt. "Blink." She reminded herself as she felt a tear in the corner of her eye. No, she wouldn't cry. Not now. She closed her deep blue eyes tight, opened them, examined her flawless face in the rearview mirror, and ran her hand through her short brown hair. She needed to think. This news would change her whole life. She searched her own eyes in the mirror.

She shook her head. She had things to do. She would think about this later. She pulled out of the parking lot. Time to go back to work. She turned on the radio. Music was sure to distract her from her thoughts. Madonna's "Papa Don't Preach" belted from the radio and mocked her. She quickly scanned through a few more channels. She didn't get past the "mama" in Abba's "Mama Mia" or "sweet baby" in "Sweet Baby James" by James Taylor. After hitting on "Let Me Be Your Baby" by Geoffrey Williams, she switched off the radio. No distraction there. Baby, Mama, Papa. Words she could do without at the moment. She blinked back tears again.

As she slowed to a stop at a red light, her cell phone rang. She glanced at the name - Marianne from the office. She groaned and blinked back another tear. Suddenly she heard her voice speaking into the phone, "Hello, Marianne, look, I'm not coming back in this afternoon. Let Dale know."

"Hi, Aerial, no problem. I was just calling to tell you there's no need to rush back. John called to change this afternoon's appointment to Monday. He got stuck in Chicago. His plane was delayed by mechanical problems."

"Okay."

"Aerial, are you all right?"

"What? Oh, yeah, fine. I've just need to take care of a few things."

"Okay. Well there's nothing else on your calendar, so that shouldn't be a problem. See you Monday."

"Yeah, Monday. Bye." She hung up, blinked back yet another tear and pulled into the parking lot at the mall.

Aerial stood outside the evening gown shop and stared. If she took a few steps, she could find out when her dress would be ready. She hesitated. *What was the point?* She turned away from the shop. Her heart refused to let her enter.

She blinked rapidly to keep her tears at bay as she walked aimlessly through the mall. She tried to push the doctor's words away, but every step she took brought into sight another reminder.

Mothers held their children's hands. Women pushed strollers. Toddlers squirmed on their mother's hips. Infants snuggled in their mama's arms.

She turned her head to the other side and saw a little girl's face pressed up against the glass of a toy store, a mother comforting a crying infant, and a small boy's delight as his mom handed him an ice cream cone. She sighed. She'd never know how those mothers must feel. She'd never experience any of those moments. She heard a tiny voice saying, "Mommy, I love you."

The child's words broke down her defenses bringing the doctor's words crashing down on her. "Aerial, the test we performed show that the infection you had several years back damaged your uterus as well as your fallopian tubes leaving considerable scar tissue. I'm sorry, Aerial, that's why you've been unable to conceive." She didn't even care what else the doctor said. She'd never have a child of her own.

"Excuse me." The words brought her attention to a lady pushing the stroller directly into her path.

"Sorry." She mumbled and fought by tears.

She hurried into the closest store determined to focus on buying clothes for her upcoming second honeymoon – provided, of course, there would be one. They planned to leave the day following their anniversary celebration for a full month in the Caribbean. She piled lightweight pants, skirts, dresses, shirts, and bathing suits into her arms, then passed them to a sales lady to put in a dressing room. Three armloads of clothes later, she stood in the dressing room mixing and matching the clothes before trying them on. She welcomed the distraction.

Forty-five minutes later she walked out of the dressing room. She carried an armload of clothing she couldn't see over. Balancing the clothes and her purse, she looked around the clothes and made her way to the counter. She groaned when she saw how long the line had become.

She shifted the clothes and looked at the line. She counted a reasonable number of heads who stood with wide distances between them. She shifted to see why they stood so far apart. Then she saw – stroller after stroller and child after child. The rest of the doctor's words played in her mind. "I'm really sorry, Aerial. I know this isn't what you wanted to hear. Natural conception just isn't a viable option. I know we were hopeful after your last visit."

"If I'd treated the infection sooner, would it have made a difference?"

"Maybe if you'd treated it in the first few weeks or maybe even within a couple of months after the rape, but as we discussed there often aren't any symptoms and the symptoms are often misdiagnosed as something much less damaging."

"I just didn't want anyone to know what happened to me. I kept trying to convince myself it never happened and that everything would be okay."

"I know, Aerial, a lot of women have the same reaction after a date rape. You really can't blame yourself. You were going through a traumatic time. It's not easy."

The sounds of the children in front of her cooing, crying, and chattering away in child language interrupted her thoughts. She shifted the clothes in her arms again and blinked back a tear. These mothers with their children represented a future she could never have. "Why did you all have to bring your children to the mall?"

She didn't even realize she said it aloud or that her tone sounded so frustrated until she saw three of the mothers turn to glare at her. Immediately, she wished she could take back the words One of the mothers stepped toward her. "What would you know about it?"

Another mother piped in, "What do you expect us to do? Abandon our children for your convenience." The venom in her voice caused Aerial to step back.

The first mother took another step toward her. Her eyes blazing, she spat her words at Aerial. "Just wait until you have children."

Aerial dropped her armload of clothes on a nearby table and ran from the store. She heard the mothers actually applaud. *How could they be so happy about her pain?* She realized even as the thought crossed her mind it was irrational. The tears erupted from her eyes as she ran through the crowd of families toward the exit. Her heart felt like it might actually explode in her chest.

She leaned against her car and tried to catch her breath and calm her tears. Her sobs impaired her vision and left her shaking so much she needed to compose herself before driving.

She looked up and saw two of the women, a blonde and brunette, from the store walking toward her. As they neared her car both women cast condescending looks her direction. Neither woman seemed to notice her tears.

The brunette muttered "Bitch!" as they passed her, and the two women laughed.

Ariel wiped the tears from her cheeks as she watched them situate their packages and toddlers in an SUV. She pulled a tissue from her purse, and wiped her nose. As she drove out of the parking lot, she imagined them bragging to their friends how they put the insensitive bitch at the mall in her place.

The Fight

Jill sat on a fallen tree at the edge of a vast meadow. She barely noticed the beauty in front of her or the faint sickly sweet odor of the rotting log beneath her. She came to this place, her favorite since early childhood, to find some peace. Instead, she felt an intense emptiness unlike anything she'd ever felt before. His words kept playing over and over in her mind. His last words. As painful as they were, she couldn't let them go. They hadn't been kind words, but she needed them now. No matter what they were. She wanted to not need them, but she needed them. She needed to not need them, but she needed them.

She shook her head to try to clear the words from her mind. How pathetic! *Why can't I let those words go? Why can't I forget them? Why can't I remember all the good and wonderful things he said to me over the years?* Because those were his last words. Because she knew she would never hear his voice again. No matter how much they hurt, those words were her last connection to him.

She pushed her hair back wiping a single tear from her right eye. No, she wouldn't cry. She'd done enough of that in the last six months. She looked around the meadow full of Spring wildflowers interspersed with growing weeds, but she barely noticed them. The clear blue sky and bright sunshine brought her no joy.

Jill closed her eyes and rubbed her hands over her protruding stomach. Just another month or so and she would be a mother. She sighed desperately wishing she'd never returned to her parents' house. She couldn't imagine raising her child even for a short time under their watchful eyes. "Oh, Little Baby, where will we go? What will we do? Daddy would have loved to be here." She looked down at her stomach. "But, of course, he never even knew about you." She wondered if things would've been different if he had.

She remembered that last night so well. She'd relived it so many times for the last six months. Ever since....

Jill left work thirty minutes late and was not happy about it. She hated staying late to finish someone else's work once again. Traffic only frustrated her that much more.

Ben still wasn't home when she arrived. She sighed, tossed her purse onto the table beside the door, and looked around the house. Her day was nowhere near finished. She sighed. She refused to let her day get to her. She didn't want to take it out on Ben. That would only lead to a fight.

After she changed into a battered navy sweat suit, she grabbed a basket of laundry and went to the laundry room to begin her evening chores.

By the time Ben arrived, she'd started steak, potatoes, and salad for dinner, folded a load of clothes, and vacuumed the entire house. She stifled a yawn as she greeted him. One look at Ben told her his day had been no better than hers. She forced a smile and tiptoed to kiss him.

Their night slowly filled with tension. Uncomfortable silence filled the moments between their stilted attempts at conversation.

She struggled to remember what the fight had been about, or at least what started it. What she remembered was that it was late, she felt overwhelmed, and just wanted to relax.

He sat on the couch and stared at the television oblivious to her constant movement. His indifference and expectations that she would do everything while he relaxed made her feel like he viewed her as a servant or at the very least didn't value that she worked as hard as he did all day.

Suddenly, they were screaming at one another. All she had wanted was time to relax, too. She remembered that. She couldn't remember what they screamed, but the anger escalated with every word.

All she remembered now were his final words as he stormed out the front door. It was like that so often. All the words in the middle got lost, but those departing words were always memorable. They stuck with her like a rock in her tennis shoe.

Jill looked around the meadow and leaned forward to pick a daisy. She brought it to her nose. The baby kicked, and she laid the daisy on top of her stomach. "That's a daisy, Little Baby. Do you like it?" She rubbed her stomach. She loved her baby, but she hadn't been able to even start thinking about names. She needed to decide on one soon.

Would things have been the same if we had known then that I was pregnant? Would he have helped me that night? Would I have all the housework go and relaxed? What would we have done differently?

She had to give him credit. He unloaded the dishwasher and stacked the dishes in the sink after they ate, but there was so much more to do. She wondered now if any of it had been all that important. At the time, it had seemed so. If she had known what the fight would ultimately cost her, she knew now that she would have just sat down and watched television with Ben.

After he stormed out of the house with his parting words, she sat in the floor and sobbed. Those words hurt her even though she knew that he didn't mean them. After a few minutes, she dried her eyes, turned on a CD, and settled into a relaxing bubble bath to wait for him to come home. He always did. They'd had much worse fights, and he often went for a drive to relieve tension.

She stepped out of the tub, put on her thick terry cloth robe, and pulled her hair out of the French braid she'd worn all day. She brushed her long brown hair. She wanted to be relaxed when Ben got home. Then they would apologize, make up, and fall asleep nestled in each other's arms.

She sat on the couch and tried to read but spent more time looking at the clock than her book. He had been gone too long. Hours had passed since he left. He never stayed gone this long. The doorbell rang. She looked up. It couldn't be good. She moved slowly toward the door. Ben's departing words echoed in her head. She opened the door and almost fainted when she saw the two police officers. They looked very serious. "Are you Mrs. Cornell?"

"Yes, sir. Is this about Ben?"

"Yes, ma'am."

She watched his lips move but she could only hear the echo of Ben's last words screaming in her head. Even without recognition of the sounds coming from the officer's mouth, she knew exactly what the he said. There was no question about their late night appearance at her door.

Ben's accident occurred as he drove home. At least that's what she wanted to believe. She wanted to believe he was on his way back to her. That would mean he didn't mean those horrible, hateful words he screamed on his way out the door.

The report stated Ben swerved to miss another car who possibly, or at least appeared to, drift very close to or over the dividing line in the highway. Witnesses disagreed as to whether or not the other car crossed the line. Ben careened over a small hill. The car rammed into a huge oak tree on a farm outside of town. He died before the ambulance arrived.

Jill looked out over the meadow. "Oh, my Little Baby, I hope you never have to hear those words. And I will do my best to teach you better than to ever utter something so cruel to another person, especially someone you love and who loves you."

She stood and walked toward her parents' home. She needed to get back on her own. She missed her independence. Moving back in with her parents had felt like her only option when she discovered she was pregnant only two weeks after Ben's death. Without his income, keeping their apartment and preparing for a baby hadn't felt possible. Besides, living with her parents had kept those last words at bay, at least at first.

It didn't seem to matter now. The words always seemed to be there. No matter how much she wanted to forget those painful words, she couldn't. They were there with her for the duration. She never shared them with anyone. They were hers and hers alone. Besides, she kept reminding herself, Ben hadn't really meant them.

As she walked through the woods, the wind whispered those last words, Ben's last words, through the trees. She saw his angry face as the words haunted her, and a tear slipped down each cheek. Oh, how she wanted to forget those words - the words, then the slamming of the door. Those last heartbreaking words screamed by the man who loved her and whom she loved with all her heart. But they were out there for always. Maybe they would fade away someday, but not today. Those words whispered, screamed, nagged at her always. "*God, why in the hell did I ever marry you, you nagging bitch? I never want to see your fucking face again.*"

All in Good Time

Anna knocked on Ian's door. When he didn't answer, she opened the door and peeked her head through the opening. She opened her mouth to speak, but stopped when she saw him sitting amidst all Julie's pictures and letters.

She stared at the evidence of the life Ian and Julie shared. He sat surrounded by a shrine – or maybe an offering - an offering that sacrificed Ian to a woman long gone. Anna looked at the pitiful remnants of a man she loved and realized she mostly felt pity for him.

She stood in the doorway and looked over Ian's shoulder. Cute, soft, petite Julie with her sparkling smile, bright green eyes, and long blond hair smiled up at a handsome, strong Ian in photo after photo. She stared at Ian. He looked nothing like those pictures anymore. In the pictures, his dark brown hair was cut short and neat, his brown eyes were filled with love for the woman he draped his muscular arm around. *When was the last time he worked out?* Anna felt tears in her eyes.

Julie had done so much for Ian. Her quiet calmness settled the playboy in him. He seemed so at peace while they were together. She wondered if he would ever find that peace again. Julie's patience and understanding helped him see his potential and stop trying to live up to the expectations of their tyrannical father who had been dead for years. Julie's success and drive noticeably inspired him in all aspects in his life.

Anna looked at the thin, broken shell in front of her with the long uncombed hair and cloudy eyes. Damn Julie to hell for doing this to him. No, that wasn't fair. He was doing this to himself. He should be able to see all the good he possessed even without her. Anna wanted him to. She wanted to make him see it. She wanted to scream at him, to shake him, to do something. He needed to see that he could have a wonderful life even without Julie, maybe even a better one. He needed to give himself a chance.

She had adored him ever since his birth. She no longer saw her brother in this thin, empty, broken shell in front of her. She wanted to force him to bring her brother back to her. *How can I do that?* She blamed Julie for having this kind of effect on her brother. It wasn't right. *How could any one human being have such a profound effect on another person?*

Steve never had that kind of effect on her. Oh, no, she wouldn't have allowed that.

Even when she loved Steve, their relationship lacked something, or maybe it contained too much of something. She never knew exactly what the problem had been just that it had been a big one. They had been married for almost four years when he left her. He hadn't even left for another woman. He'd just gotten "tired off the monotony of their relationship." He hadn't even said that in person but in a note he left her after cleaning out their bank accounts while she was at work.

If he hadn't taken all their money, she wouldn't have even cared that he left. Toward the end of their relationship she had even begun to find his lanky body, long dirty blond hair, and dark eyes less and less attractive, at times, even disgusting. She sighed. Steve wasn't even worth the trouble it took to think about him. She couldn't remember one happy memory they created together. Certainly nothing to make her feel compelled to sit and stare at pictures of their life together.

She looked at pictures of Ian and Julie at the beach, in the mountains, lounging in the backyard, and entertaining their numerous friends. She shook her head looking at the pictures of the beautiful apartment Ian and Julie shared the last two months of their life together.

Anna couldn't believe Ian moved back in with their mother after Julie. She heard that little voice in her head telling her she did the same thing. Her situation was different. After all Steve had wiped out her finances. Julie certainly hadn't done that to Ian. Besides, Anna was saving for a house not running from life. She hoped she wasn't fooling herself. That didn't matter. She needed to do something about Ian.

"Ian." When he continued to stare at the pictures, she raised her voice. "Ian!"

"What, Anna? I'm busy." His voice dripped with annoyance.

"No, you're not. You're wallowing, Ian."

He turned his blank stare to her face without a word. She walked toward him and started gathering the pictures, letters, and memorabilia. Suddenly she heard a strange sound from her brother, a mixture of an animal's scream of pain and a five-year old's shriek, "Mine."

As they struggled for the items in her hands, he jerked a heavy wooden duck on skis from her hands and somehow it landed a thud against her temple. She wasn't sure if he hit her intentionally or accidentally. "Anna, put down my Julie. Put it down now. All of it. Put it down. You don't know what you're doing. Give me my Julie. You don't know what you're doing."

"Yes, I do, Ian." She rubbed her temple. "It's time to get on with your life. Julie's gone. She's not coming back. We all lose people we love. We have to get on with life."

"Fuck you, Anna. Julie didn't leave me, and you know it. She's not Steve." His tone sounded cold enough to freeze a volcano.

"She's gone, Ian."

"No, Anna, she's dead. There's a difference."

"Ian, she's still gone. She's not coming back."

He started to cry. "I know that, Anna. That's just it. She's never coming back. That idiot took her from me. How dare he? He had no right to do that to her!"

"Ian, she gave up. She could've fought."

"Fought, Anna? Fought what? The AIDS he gave her when he raped her? Huh, Anna? Is that what you mean? She could've fought AIDS along with the nightmares and the fears and the mental anguish of having everything good in her life tainted. Is that what you mean Anna? She could've fought AIDS? How was she going to do that? She was already worn out and sick from everything else. So you tell me, how was she going to fight AIDS, Anna?"

"There are ways, Ian. Medications, lifestyle changes…."

"They only prolong. He killed her when he raped her. A part of her died that night anyway. And then to find out so quickly that he had infected her…." His voice trailed off.

"Ian, just be thankful the two of you were careful."

As if he hadn't even heard her, he went on. "And he knew it. He knew he had AIDS. He even said he wanted to give it to her, to make her suffer for breaking up with him ten fucking years ago. Long before he even got it. The asshole."

"Ian,…."

"Just get out, Anna. Don't tell me how lucky I am again. Until you go through it, I don't want to hear about it." He took her arm and pushed her from the room. "Get out. I have nothing left to say to you." She opened her mouth, but he put up his hand. "And I definitely don't want to hear anything you have to say. Go fix someone else. Avoid your own problems at all cost, and stay the hell out of mine. I don't need you. Not now, not ever."

She stood there until he grabbed the last photo from her hand and slammed the door shut. She listened as he sobbed behind the closed door. She reached for the knob but heard his voice, firm and cold. "Don't even think about it, Anna. Go away."

Anna closed her eyes and felt a rush of loss wash over her. Ian had a point; she had no idea what it felt like to have the kind of love he and Julie had shared. She doubted she ever would. She sighed.

She remembered what Julie said to her when Steve left her, and whispered those words to Ian's closed door. "All in good time. All in good time, Little Brother."

Four Walls

Stella stepped into the room where she'd lost herself, the last place she remembered being the girl she remembered before she became... this, whatever this was.

She looked into the mirror she'd looked into so often over those years and the face looking back at her looked nothing like the face she'd looked at just that morning in a different mirror in a hotel room not far from this place, this place she'd vowed never to set foot in again. The face looking back at her held an innocence she couldn't remember ever feeling, but must have. The jaded face she'd looked at earlier felt more disconnected than even this innocent face.

She turned away from the mirror and walked around the sparsely furnished room. An old metal bed frame leaned against the wall. She remembered putting that bed, or at least one very much like it, together each Fall semester. She noted the bed was too damaged to put together anymore. There was no mattress. She hoped the mattress she'd slept on had been burned to ashes or shredded into confetti-sized pieces. Anything to destroy the memories it held.

She looked toward the built-in shelves she'd so carefully displayed her life on in those days. The built-in dressers that had housed her clothing, dishes, and odds and ends now stood as empty as they were at the beginning of each school year. Everything she owned, with the exception of her car, contained in this small room.

Somehow it felt smaller than it had then.

She blinked back a tear and opened the closet doors. Looking inside she saw nothing but an empty rod and a shelf in each. Even the racks on the doors where she'd hung her towels were gone. It felt oddly like her room and not like her room.

It was nothing like she remembered and yet still felt so familiar. So much had happened between these four walls. Her entire life had changed between these four walls. Her faith in people had been demolished between these four walls. Her sense of self had been lost between these four walls.

She walked to the window and stared out at a mostly empty parking lot and the buildings in the distance. Trees dotting the landscape blocked views she'd easily seen all those years ago. She let her mind wander back to the days when she'd embraced this room, when she'd felt like life was a huge adventure just waiting for her to explore, when she'd felt like nothing could ever stop her.

She remembered happy moments and making friends. She remembered laughter and silliness. She remembered music and dancing. She remembered relationships lost and gained. She remembered studying until she fell asleep on her books and waking up with her highlighter in her hair. She remembered her excitement over having her own life.

Then...

She didn't want to remember that, but how could she not? That moment had defined her for so very long. That moment when she felt friendly hands turn to unwelcome touches, when her pleas for him to stop had been ignored, when her tears were laughed at... when her best friend turned worst foe.

She felt a tear slide down her cheek and looked back toward the mirror again and saw both her faces reflected back at her. She loved the girl she'd been. She loved the woman she'd become. Yet somehow between the two was a woman she couldn't bear to look in the eye, a woman she didn't recognize, a woman she almost hated.

Stella sighed, turned the key over in her hand, turned back to the window one last time. Life had a way of taking you along for the ride whether you were ready or not. Hers certainly had never stopped long enough to let her catch up to it. Life didn't stop when she felt like she couldn't take another step forward. So many days in a daze that left her uncertain of her past or her present or her future. She'd cried far too many tears over what she'd lost until she'd found her footing and stopped letting fear rule her every single move.

It wasn't always easy and often she still fought her old demons. The anxiety, the fear, the inability to trust popped back into her life and created havoc. At least these days, she saw it before it completely destroyed her, right? Sometimes it felt like she was only fooling herself.

With her hand on the window, she leaned forward and touched her forehead to the cold glass and let her tears flow freely. Her body wracked with sobs and her nose ran, but she didn't stop to check her ugly release. She didn't care. She'd come here to face her past and experience whatever that brought up. So she would. She sank to the floor and looked up.

Four walls surrounded her. It had been home. Then it had felt like a prison. Now she looked around as the tears flowed and she released the part of her this room had stolen. It suddenly just felt like four walls. She thought of all the people who'd lived in this room since she had. She thought of how they all had their own stories, too... Some good, some bad, but each feeling deeply personal and probably somehow still universal.

She'd always thought of this room as hers, but all those bodies, all those personalities, all those people who had moved through it before and after her had made her one of a crowd. She wiped her nose with the back of her hand and hoped each of them had more good experiences than bad ones in this room. She hoped none of them experienced that one bad moment that tainted all the good ones for all time.

Ten minutes later she passed the demolition crew as the wrecking ball made contact with the building, she wiped away her tears, straightened her shoulders, and didn't even bother to glance over her shoulder.

Inside those four walls, she'd found the girl she was inside the woman she'd become and in doing so had freed them both from a prison they'd never deserved to inhabit.

Stripped

Martini stepped out of the Bellagio employee entrance and looked for her sister's car. Whiskey waved. Martini hurried over and opened the car door. "Hey, Martini, how was your day?"

"Same as usual only half as long. What did you do today?"

"Worked out and slept."

Whiskey pulled into the street. Martini watched the traffic as Whiskey drove. Her mind wandered as it had many times throughout the day. "Whiskey, do you ever wonder why Mom and Dad named us after alcohol?"

"Dad named us. Mom had nothing to do with it."

"What?"

"He told me a few days before he died."

"Really?"

"Yeah, he named us after his drink of choice the night we were each conceived. His three phases of alcohol – Martini, Whiskey, and Vodka. Go figure."

"You've got to be kidding. What was he thinking?" She rolled her eyes. "Did he plan for us to all be strippers from birth?"

"I doubt that. He just loved his booze so he named us after what he loved."

"Did Vodka know?"

"Not as far as I know."

"Do you think if he'd named her something normal she'd still be alive?"

"I doubt we'll ever know the answer to that. She had problems, but I'm sure the teasing didn't help."

"I miss her."

"So do I."

Silence permeated the car as they remembered Vodka, their youngest sister. Vodka had always been the most sensitive of the three sisters. Growing up in their home, sensitivity was dangerous. Their father loved his alcohol more than anything else. He vacillated between extreme niceness and cruelty. They almost preferred him drinking but definitely not drunk. On either side of his drinking, he was mean. Their mother worked two jobs, held everything together and had neither the time nor the inclination to be nurturing. She made no secret that her life would've been perfect if she wasn't "tied to this drunk and these brats."

One spring day they came home from school to discover their mom left in search of the perfect life she wanted. She left each of them a note on their pillows. Each was a variation of a declaration of her love for them, that staying had become too difficult, too depressing, how she needed something more. In each letter, she extolled a few abstract virtues of the girls, and then added a note about how she hoped they wouldn't make the same mistakes she did. They compared the letters pained that she hadn't known them well enough to actually individualize the letters. They never heard from her again.

Almost two years later, Martini picked up her two younger sisters from their friend's house. "Dad's dead. We've got to get out of town or we'll end up in foster homes."

"What do you mean? How can Dad be dead?" Vodka's eyes shined with tears.

"Dad's drinking buddy, Butch, called and said Dad stumbled into the bar around three this afternoon already drunk. An hour and three drinks later, he stood up, threw a fifty on the table, walked to the door, opened it, and collapsed half in and half out of the bar. Probably a heart attack, but who knows?" She shrugged. "Butch said that in cases like this, the kids usually end up in foster care and not always together. It's even worse because we don't even know where Mom went. I took the money Dad hid in his gun safe. I packed up our things – as much as I could get in the car."

"Where are we going?" Whiskey's eyes were emotionless, her

expression hard. No tears there.

"I don't know, but I don't want to be separated from you two."

"We should go to a big city. It'll be easier to get lost and find work. Maybe San Francisco or Los Angeles." Whiskey smiled. "No Vegas. Las Vegas. That's where we should go."

"Las Vegas. Of course, Dad always said Vegas was the place to go." Martini smiled. "I should be able to find work pretty easily there. They always need waitresses, entertainers, and stuff like that. Besides I dance really well. I can probably get a job in a show or something. You two can finish high school. We'll make this work."

Whiskey and Vodka exchanged looks. "Martini, what about you? You still have a year of high school left. You're only sixteen." Whiskey stared at her.

"I'll be seventeen next month. I don't need a high school diploma to dance or to waitress."

Vodka barely spoke throughout the two-day drive to Las Vegas. She pouted. She left behind a boyfriend and a best friend. She cried. The only time she spoke was to bemoan their father's death and curse their mother for deserting them.

The sisters found a dirty, bug infested apartment and enrolled Whiskey and Vodka in a high school that didn't look much better than their apartment and didn't ask many questions. Martini and Whiskey found waitress jobs at a tiny diner with a 1950s vibe that might actually have been open since the 1950s across the street from their apartment. Vodka seldom spoke or shared anything about her life with them.

Before Whiskey and Vodka started school, the money they made from the diner, even supplemented by the money they brought with them, came nowhere near meeting their needs. With Whiskey working fewer hours so she could attend school, money became even tighter. Martini bought a fake driver's license from one of her customers at the diner, so she could get a second job as a waitress in a strip joint a couple of blocks away where they didn't ask questions.

Once in school, Vodka withdrew even deeper into herself, barely ate or slept, and became edgier every day. She didn't make new friends and showed no desire to try. She locked herself in her room for hours at a time – sometimes from the time she arrived home from school until she left for school the next morning.

Though Whiskey sensed something wasn't quite right, she was too tired between school and work to talk to Vodka or bring it to Martini's attention. Martini wasn't around enough to notice Vodka become increasingly morose.

About seven months after their move to Las Vegas, Martini rushed through the door already stripping out of her diner waitress uniform, so she could shower the smell of grilled cheese, hamburger grease, and French fries out of her hair and skin before starting her shift at the strip club. She knocked on Vodka's door but there was no answer. "Vodka, I haven't seen you in two weeks. Please open the door. I only have a few minutes. Come on. Open up."

She rapped her knuckles on the door again. When Vodka didn't answer, she sighed and turned into the bathroom. She pulled back the shower curtain and gasped as she covered her mouth with her hand. Vodka sat in a tub full of water, her eyes closed, and her head drooping. Martini shook her shoulder and winced at Vodka's clammy skin. "What the hell...? Vodka, what have you done? Vodka?"

Martini collapsed back against the wall between the tub and the toilet. She failed her baby sister. *What could I have done? What did I miss? What the hell happened?* She worked so hard to keep their family together. Whiskey found her there ten minutes later with tears streaming down her cheeks.

Martini and Whiskey somehow survived the police questioning, the investigation, and the ruling of the death as an overdose of illegal drugs, possible suicide.

A hazy cloud surrounded them as they planned and attended Vodka's funeral. Very few of Vodka's classmates or teachers showed up, and those who did didn't really seem to know her. School records showed Vodka skipped more classes than she attended resulting in her once stellar grades becoming failing grades.

Neither Whiskey nor Martini could sleep in the apartment, so they moved to another cheap, bug infested apartment – this time a one-bedroom to save money.

A few weeks after Vodka's death, Martini started filling in for sick and no-show strippers. She made three times as much money as a stripper than as a waitress, so she stripped more often and waitressed less often. She barely noticed when she transitioned from waitress to stripper.

Whiskey graduated from high school. College wasn't an option, so they never discussed it. Within six months, Whiskey moved from her job at the diner to one in a local steakhouse. When they couldn't pull in enough money to make ends meet, she took shifts as a waitress at the strip joint where Martini worked. Eventually Whiskey took a stripping job at a club down the street from where Martini stripped.

Over the next four years, the sisters moved from one strip joint to another occasionally attempting to take other jobs but the money kept drawing them back. Somehow along the way they convinced themselves it was the only thing they did well. They prided themselves on never resorting to prostitution. They developed some semblance of real lives complete with savings accounts, dreams of pursuing their true ambitions, and the occasional boyfriend.

Then one of Martini's customers knocked her off the stage in a drunken rage breaking her leg and somehow slicing her from her hip bone, diagonal across her buttocks, half way down her left thigh. The scar was unsightly and the medical bills and forced time off had almost left her homeless.

Whiskey refused to abandon Martini after all Martini sacrificed for Vodka and her. She let her move in with her and helped her get a job as a topless waitress where she stripped. At the time, paying the bills had been her utmost concern as it had been since she was sixteen. She thought once she healed she would go back to stripping but the scar was too pronounced. It glowed under the stage lights. Customers found it unappealing, and she felt self-conscious about it.

Neither held dreams of "Prince Charming" whisking them away from it all anymore.

Whiskey parked the car outside the strip joint – gentleman's club as the places that wanted to attract a *classier* clientele called themselves. Regardless of what the clubs called themselves or their employees – gentleman's club, exotic dancer, entertainer - it still consisted of taking their clothes off for money, drunk men groping them with mirth, being treated like playthings devoid of thoughts or feelings, and going home reeking of smoke and booze without ever smoking a cigarette or taking a drink. She looked at Martini. "I've been thinking about it all, too. A lot lately. Everything that brought us to this point and how much longer we can do this."

"I didn't say a word."

"You didn't have to. I've seen it in your eyes for a while. The way you pour over the accounts week after week. I know you're trying to figure out how we'll survive once we're too old for this crap." She pointed toward the club. "I'm tired of it, too."

"But I don't want to go back to living in bug infested, uncleanable hovels either.

"We're still young, Martini. I've been looking into college. We would both qualify for grants and there are always loans. We could keep doing this for a little while then transition into better jobs even if they pay less."

"You can do that. I didn't finish high school. Remember?"

"But you can fix that. You can get your GED or apply for special consideration. Martini, we have to get out of this life before another drunk does something even worse than causing you to fall. Your injuries were severe, but next time one of these idiots could beat or rape or kill one of us."

"We've tried other jobs. We always come back to this. Sometimes I feel like it's all I can do. All I'm good for."

"Martini, that's just not true. You can do anything you set your mind to. Look how you took care of Vodka and me. You kept our family together."

"I didn't do enough for Vodka. She's dead. We lost her and it's my fault, Whiskey. You know it is."

"No, I don't. Vodka had problems. We were all kids. We weren't equipped to deal with those kinds of problems. I read her journal. Her problems went back years, even before Mom left. The drugs were either her self-medicating or she committed suicide. Based on her journal either is entirely possible. We'll never know."

"I should've seen it coming."

"We were trying to survive. We're not perfect. We did everything we could."

Martini closed her eyes, held her breath for a count of eight, and slowly exhaled before she spoke. "Whiskey, we have to go in now or we'll be late."

"Will you think about it, Martini? We've got to change our lives. We deserve better than spending our nights being groped by strange men. You work two jobs and I start a second job next week. All we do is work. We're still struggling just to survive."

Martini blinked back tears. "You found another job?"

"Yes, I did. It doesn't pay much, but maybe I can learn something. I'll be an inventory clerk at a bookstore on campus. It's part-time, but I'll be able to get a free class out of it. But you're right, let's go in before we're late."

They walked to the door in silence. Just before they reached the door, Martini grabbed Whiskey's arm. "Wait a sec. How long have you felt this way?"

"A long time. Feels like forever."

"Wow, I never knew. You always seemed to almost like this stuff. You never said anything about wanting something different. I never understood it because I spend most of my time daydreaming about finding a way out of this life, but I never thought I could."

"That's because you always focused on taking care of Vodka and me. You felt responsible for us to the exclusion of having your own life at all."

"Actually, I just gave up. You developed a plan. Do you really think we can do it?"

Martini allowed herself to consider possibilities for the first time since they left Boise. She felt hopeful. She dared to dream. The possibility seemed so far away, so remote. "So, Whiskey, what do you want to study?"

"I'm not sure. I know I want to help kids, so maybe psychology, social work, or something along those lines. I thought I'd take a few classes before deciding. What about you?"

"I think I'd like to be a lawyer. It's what I wanted before all this happened."

"I remember."

They stepped into the dark bar and headed down the stairs to prepare for work. As Whiskey slipped into her businesswoman costume for her "businesswoman gone wild" act, and Martini slipped off her shirt and on her shiny, star-shaped pasties and a black skirt specially cut to hide her scars while revealing enough to get the patrons to spend more and tip well.

Martini spent her evening laughing at jokes she didn't find amusing, smiling at men who disgusted her, and pretending being groped by strangers was not only acceptable but desired.

After Whiskey's last set turning the conservative, staid businesswoman into a stripper pole humping sex toy, Martini followed her down the stairs desperately wanting to shower the night off her body. Whiskey's expression screamed that she felt the same way. They quickly and quietly changed back into their street clothes.

As they stepped out of the strip joint, they heard all the usual drunken lewd offers. Martini had become numb to it over the years, but that night for the first time in a long time, she flinched as a flush of anger spread over her.

"Come on, Babe, I got something for you."

"Let's fuck. You know you want to."

"I'll fuck you both real good."

It was usually just so much chatter. This time she turned to Whiskey. "Damn, I can't take this anymore. Let's do it."

Whiskey took her arm and quickly steered her to the car. "Just ignore them, Martini."

Martini laughed. "That's not what I meant. Let's quit these jobs. We really do deserve better than this. I don't care if things get harder. I need my dignity back. I can't even remember when I last had any. We can live on campus to save money."

"When do you want to quit?"

"I just did."

They turned and extended their middle fingers toward the strip club, collapsed in giggles, and climbed in the car.

Neither Martini nor Whiskey looked back as they sped down the empty street toward their futures shining bright in the distance.

Missing

Tears streamed down Andrea's face as she pressed the button to disconnect the phone call. She couldn't believe the news. Her best friend, Liza, was nowhere to be found. Questions swarmed Andrea's mind. *Had she disappeared of her own free will? Where was she? What was she doing? Was she hurt? Or was she sitting on some beach basking in the sun's heat and thinking only of herself? Or had she taken off with some guy she had just met? Who knew?* Someone, somewhere, must know.

Liza was always unpredictable. She never let the world see her unhappiness, but, on the other hand, she hated to be alone. Andrea flopped down on the sofa and looked around the apartment slowly looking for anything she might have missed. They'd been roommates since their freshman year of college. She quickly calculated the years in her mind – eight. *Had it really been eight years?*

Her gaze stopped when she noticed a photo taken recently of the two of them. What a contrast they made, not just physically but in their personalities as well. Liza had long bleach-blond hair that she loved to let fly loose and unruly. Her big blue eyes always twinkled with just a bit too much trust. Her body was too thin, a result of her apathy toward food. Andrea looked at herself in the photo. She wore her dark hair pulled back in a tight, perfect ponytail just like today and her brown eyes appeared serious, and, if she would admit it, a bit cynical.

Their cat jumped onto the sofa breaking into her thoughts. "Damn it, Stray, where could she be? She would never leave us now, would she?" She ran her hand down the cat's back.

Stray gazed at her, cocked his head to the side, and turned to walk back under her hand.

Andrea had grown used to Liza's abundance of generosity and big heart. After all, that's how Stray came into their lives. Liza found him as a kitten. She had brought him home not being able to stand the thought of "the poor little kitty starving to death all by itself by the side of the road." Andrea had been furious, but now she couldn't imagine life without Stray, just like she couldn't imagine life without Liza. No, she mustn't think that way. She wouldn't let herself. There was hope.

She dug Liza's address book out of her cluttered desk and placed it on the coffee table in front of her. She needed to call all of Liza's friends and favorite haunts. *How dare she put all of them through this?* Andrea planned to give her hell when she strolled later.

When Liza's Mom called the previous day, Andrea failed to hide her surprise. She tried to reassure Liza's Mom only to learn Liza received a phone call that upset her so much she left without giving an explanation and barely managed to eke out a "Love you. Bye." as she left.

Andrea called Liza's boyfriend the previous night and learned from his roommate that Liza's boyfriend had broken up with her over two weeks earlier. He and his assistant had been in Barbados since then. *Why didn't Liza tell me?* Liza never kept secrets from her.

Liza's behavior hadn't changed, not anything she noticed anyway. Maybe she missed something. Maybe Liza needed some time to herself. Liza would never just disappear. She wouldn't lie to her parents. Something went wrong somewhere between their house and the apartment.

As she picked up the phone and dialed the first number in Liza's address book, she sighed and reminded herself to just start at the beginning. She sat at the kitchen table, sipped coffee and dialed number after number. She called her way through a third of the alphabet by noon. Not bad for two hours of phone calls. Liza knew a lot of people, a lot more than Andrea knew she knew. She slapped some almond butter and blackberry jelly on two slices of whole wheat bread and pushed them together. She lifted the sandwich to her mouth taking a bite between each phone call until it was all gone. She looked at the empty plate. She'd been so preoccupied she hadn't even tasted it. She picked up the cordless phone and moved to the porch of their small apartment seeking a place less confining.

She called all of the numbers listed in the book before dinner time. No one had seen or heard from Liza since she left her parents' house. No one had even talked to her while she visited them. She called all of Liza's haunts with no luck. She called the police and talked to the missing persons department. Some man with a tired, bored voice promised to send an officer over to take a statement and get a photograph.

Andrea realized she still wore her pajamas. She jumped in the shower where stayed barely long enough for the water hit her shoulders. She pulled on a pair of denim shorts and a faded sweatshirt as the doorbell sounded. "Sure cut that close." She mumbled as she walked to the door.

She squared her shoulders and let out a slow breath before she opened the door. She refused to let emotion take over and further complicate the situation. She cared deeply for Liza, but she refused to give in to her fears. She needed to help find her.

The detectives asked her a series of questions about Liza's habits, friends, and family. Andrea struggled to keep her composure. She looked from one detective to the other. Detective Michaels, a petite African American female with short, neat hair and sympathetic brown eyes, listened intently as Andrea answered her questions. Detective Buffett, a muscular white man standing more than six feet tall with short blond hair and disinterested brown eyes, appeared more interested in the apartment than the conversation. She looked from one to the other. She struggled to remember their names.

Detective Buffett walked around the apartment and looked at all their stuff. He closely examined the photos on display. He occasionally asked for clarification or interjected a question. When Stray approached him, he offered his hand for the cat to sniff without so much as a change of expression.

When they asked to see Liza's room, Andrea hesitated because

Liza valued her privacy. She'd be mad enough at her for taking the address book from the room, but the detectives needed entrance in order to do their job.

Andrea stood in the room and watched every move they made. Finally, she worked up the nerve to ask the question she wanted to ask since they arrived. "How likely is it that we'll find her?"

Detective Michaels turned around and looked at her. "It's really hard to say. It depends on a lot. Liza could have just taken off for a few days without telling anyone. In that case, she'll come back on her own."

"And if she didn't?"

"Well, there's really no way of knowing. Look, I'm going to be honest with you. She's actually been missing for quite a while. The longer someone is missing, the more difficult it becomes to find them. That's why you have to give us everything you've got that might help us. Can you think of anyone she's fought with recently? Anyone at all?"

"Only her boyfriend, but I just found out about that today. According to his brother, he's been in Barbados for almost three weeks, and he's not due back for at least another week."

"Where does he live?"

"He and his brother live together. I'll get the address for you. It's in her address book."

After the police left with a number of things from Liza's room, a picture of Liza, Liza's hairbrush, and her address book, Andrea sank back on the sofa and called Liza's Mom.

Andrea searched Liza's room. She needed to find a clue, something. Maybe the police missed something.

She searched until Liza's parents arrived an hour and a half later.

Liza's parents settled into Liza's room while Andrea cooked dinner. They exchanged some idle chitchat, but soon silence hung heavy in the room. Finally, Andrea suggested they all try to sleep. They needed clear minds to think about the situation.

They awoke after a restless night and ate breakfast in relative silence as they waited for news. Nothing new. No word. Liza's parents went to the police station while Andrea went to see a few people she thought might have heard from Liza. No luck.

Liza's parents returned late in the afternoon. Liza's mother's gray bun had slipped from its tight knot at the back of her head. Her red-rimmed blue eyes projected her despondency. Liza's father looked no better. His striking features were drawn tight in worry. His hazel eyes searched everything in sight. He ran his hand through his rumpled gray hair.

Andrea tried to imagine what they felt, but she failed. Andrea felt selfish for thinking of her own loss, her best friend, as she looked at their faces. How they loved Liza!

Liza always talked about her happy childhood with so much delight - carefree and fun as she told everyone with a huge smile. Her parents spoiled her, and she knew it. She even seemed proud of it at times. Her parents also sheltered her from life's harsh realities. She knew little of the world, of crime, violence, and pain. This left her not only trusting but gullible. She appeared truly blessed. Nothing bad ever happened to her. Maybe that had changed.

Andrea sighed.

Andrea's family had never been close, so she'd reached adulthood trusting no one. She doubted she'd recognize trust if someone wrapped it up and presented it with a pretty little bow on top. She questioned everything and everyone. She had few friends. Andrea grew up with all the harsh realities of the world. Her mother married more times than she could remember and dated even more. She witnessed drug use first hand, suffered through abandonment and neglect, worked her way out of that world, and never looked back. No one would notice if *she* disappeared. She lost contact with her mother years earlier, and no one ever came looking for her. A tear slipped from her eye as she once again considered her selfishness. She needed to do *something* to help Liza's parents.

Liza's parents retired to Liza's room rest at Andrea's insistence. She watched as their view of the world crashed around them. They lived the protected life they provided their daughter. Andrea collapsed on the sofa and searched her mind for something to be of assistance, to herself, to Liza's parents, to help find Liza. Anything. She jumped when she heard a knock on the door. She peeked through the peephole and opened the door. "Detective Michaels? It's awfully late. Do you have news?"

"I'm not sure. Are her parents still here?"

"Yes, of course. They're resting at the moment."

"We think we've found her car, but the license plate missing as are the registration papers. Do you think you could ID it, or do we need to disturb her parents?"

"What's going on?" The voice came from behind Andrea. They both turned toward the sound and saw the ashen faces of Liza's parents.

Detective Michaels filled them in. Then they went to the police station to identify the car.

It was Liza's car.

The police had found Liza's car by the side of the road considered the country route into town. Andrea guessed Liza drove through the tree-lined roads to calm her mind because Liza often told everyone just how relaxing she found that route. It appeared her car had broken down leaving Liza stranded miles from town on the sparsely travelled road.

Detectives Michaels and Buffett settled Liza's parents and Andrea around a conference room table and offered them coffee. The detectives sat down and opened their notepads. Both jotted down notes as they asked questions.

Detective Michaels started. "Was Liza carrying a cell phone?"

Andrea spoke as Liza's parents shook their heads no. "Hers broke a couple of weeks ago. She hadn't replaced it yet."

Detective Buffett asked, "Would she have walked to find help?"

"I don't know." Liza's Dad spoke and the others shrugged, so he continued. "I always told her to stay with the car until help came. If it seemed like there was no one coming, she might have, but I think she would've gone to someone's house."

Liza's Mom's eyes shone with hope. "Did you check with the people who lived nearby?"

"We have officers out doing that right now. So far no one has seen her." Detective Michaels voice sounded far too calm to Andrea.

"Would she have accepted a ride with a stranger?" Detective Buffet looked right at Liza's Dad.

"Absolutely not." Liza's Mom answered sounding indignant.

Andrea looked down because she wasn't so sure Liza's Mom was right. She kept the thought to herself, but when she looked up saw Detective Michaels raise an eyebrow in her direction. Still she said nothing.

Detective Michaels turned to Liza's parents. "If she had tried to walk for help would she have cut through the woods or stayed on the road?"

"I can't imagine she would cut through the woods unless she knew where she was going." Liza's dad spoke softly. "But I can't be sure."

"Could she have been meeting someone out there?" Detective Buffett's expression remained noncommittal.

Andrea wondered how he managed to show no emotion as she answered. "I doubt it. She just takes that route when she wants to think. She finds it more peaceful than the Interstate."

"Who would she have called if she got to a phone that night?" Detective Michaels asked.

All three agreed that she most likely would have called Andrea because they found the car closer to Andrea than her parents' house.

Andrea listened to the officers explain their plans to search the area. She nodded when they requested something - a piece of clothing, a sheet, a towel, anything - with Liza's scent on it for the dogs. Her thoughts wandered. Something felt wrong. Then it hit her. "Where's her luggage?"

The room became very quiet as all eyes looked toward Andrea. Detective Michaels spoke first. "Luggage?"

"Yes, there should have been luggage in the car, right?" She looked at Liza's father.

"Well, yes, she had two suitcases with her when she left our house. She'd been visiting for a little over a week."

"There was no luggage in the car. Would she have tried to carry it with her if she went for help?"

"Not likely. It would have been too heavy for that."

Detective Michaels rubbed her temples and looked around the room at the expectant faces. Andrea saw pain and empathy in her eyes. She wondered if this case reminded Detective Michaels of another case or perhaps an experience from her own life.

Andrea returned to the apartment alone while Liza's parents spent some more time with the police answering questions and providing information. She stood in the doorway for a long while before she stepped into Liza's room. She'd never snooped in

Liza's journals before, but they needed a clue. Liza started a new journal the night before she left for her parents' house. If Liza met someone maybe there would be clue in the thoughts she'd written in her last journal. They'd already tried that with the phone records including the call Liza received just before she left her parents. The call originated from a payphone near the apartment Liza and Andrea shared.

Liza kept her journals locked in a trunk in her closet. Andrea found the key in the nightstand and unlocked the trunk. Her hand shook. She read the most current dates first. She found a few names she didn't recognize. She wrote them down to give to Detective Michaels. "Oh, Liza, don't be mad at me for invading your private thoughts." She muttered as she placed the journal on the table and reached for the phone just as it rang.

Detective Michaels launched right into the purpose for her call. "Andrea, have you found something we can use for the search? A piece of clothing or something."

"Huh? Oh, yeah. Sure. Look I also remembered Liza keeps a box of journals. I opened it. There are a few names I don't recognize in her most recent one. First names only, but I thought you might want to take a look at them."

"Sure, I'll be right over.

Detective Michaels sealed the scarf from Liza's closet in a bag to preserve the scent. She requested Andrea's help with Liza's journals, so they could make sense of what they read. They read journals from the previous six months. The journals didn't provide much more than a short list of names of people Andrea didn't know. Mostly, Liza documented her routine and expressed her feelings about each day.

The search continued. Days passed. Liza's parents returned to their home. Andrea returned to work. Weeks passed. The police found nothing.

Every day Andrea hoped she'd come home and find Liza curled up with Stray on the couch. Every day she found Stray curled up on Liza's perfectly made bed instead.

Andrea began to wonder if maybe Liza just left. Liza's boyfriend returned from Barbados. The police questioned and released him. They found no clues.

Andrea appreciated Detective Michaels tenacity and weekly

progress, or lack thereof, reports, but her hope weakened more every day.

The police checked Liza's financials and discovered charges on her Visa card since her disappearance. Security cameras from two states showed a woman with a build similar to Liza using the card. Then the charges stopped.

A postcard arrived in Andrea's mail exactly one year after Liza went missing. Andrea stared at the teddy bears on the front sitting around a tea party. The block on the postcard for writing a message was completely blank. The sender addressed it to their apartment address but included no name or a signature.

Andrea drove straight to the police department. As she handed the postcard to Detective Michaels, she blurted. "We have to find her. Liza hated tea parties, and she despised teddy bears even more."

The sympathetic look on Detective Michael's gave her chills while telling her all she needed to know. The case was cold…

Liza would remain missing…

You Have No Right

Misty spread the papers she'd brought with her across the conference table in Shane's office. Shane walked in carrying another stack of papers fresh from the copier. She liked working with Shane. His intelligence and attention for detail complemented her creativity and approachability. They worked well together even though his penitent for working with paper copies instead of digital struck her as old-fashioned and wasteful.

They arranged and rearranged the papers as they discussed the best way to present their material. Shane bumped into Misty once, twice, thrice... His arm brushed against her breast as he leaned over her. His leg bumped her buttock as he walked around her. Each time she moved away and convinced herself it was accidental.

Once they found the right order for the papers, they sat down to review the draft again and make sure everything was in the right place. Shane moved closer to her. He inched his chair closer and closer and then closer again until their knees were touching. She casually moved away without saying a word.

Shane stood up and stretched. He squeezed her shoulders as he said. "We're making some great progress, but maybe we should plan on a late night."

Misty stood, slipped away from his hands, and moved away from him. "I can't. I have to get home. Mitch and I have dinner plans with his boss."

Shane turned toward her and glanced down toward his crotch.

"That's too bad." She noticed the slight bulge in his pants and turned away disgusted. "I really need to go now.

A few days later, Misty sat at her desk going over the proposed changes to the presentation. The very proposal Shane had praised just days before was now covered in red marks and suggestions for changes. She sighed. Things he'd praised her for now were no longer acceptable.

A few minutes later, Shane called her. "Misty, how's the presentation coming?"

"I'm working on the changes you suggested."

"Good."

"I don't understand why you want to change some of these things. You gave them high praise the other day."

"That was the other day. I changed my mind."

"Okay. Well, I should have the changes made within the hour."

"Fine. One hour. Then bring the presentation in here, and we'll go over it again."

"That's only fifteen minutes before quitting time."

"Well, we'll have to hurry or stay late. This is too important to wait."

"Fine. I'll bring it over as soon as I'm finished."

Misty typed the changes he'd suggested, emailed it to Shane, and printed two copies. She knew he'd insist on going over a printed copy. He always did. She glanced at her watch. It'd only taken her forty minutes. Maybe she would get out of the office on time.

She knocked on Shane's door. "All done."

He glanced up from the papers he was reading and waved her into the room. She walked in, carefully leaving the door open, and sat down across from him. He stood and walked over to close the door. "That's better." He said as he patted her shoulder and took a seat in the chair next to her instead of behind his desk.

Misty dropped her shoulder away from his hand and handed him the papers. "Here. I hope this is better."

He dropped the papers on the desk. "I'm sure it's fine."

She looked down at her copy and said. "I know how important it is we land this account."

"That can wait."

"What?" She looked up surprised.

"I think you should wear that red dress you wore last week when we give the presentation."

"What red dress?"

"The one that hugs your curves so nicely but isn't so sexy as to offend the women at the presentation."

"Are you kidding me?"

"No, not at all. You look great in that red dress."

"I meant. Why are you telling me what to wear? It sounds like you're trying to use my body to land an account?"

"When you put it that way, it sounds bad." He smiled, shifted in the chair, and rearranged his pants. "I just want you to look your best. It *is* an important account."

"Shane, this is inappropriate. You can't tell me what to wear or ask me to dress a certain way to influence our clients."

"Whoa, Misty, hold on there. You took me all wrong. I'm just trying to make sure we both put forth our best."

Misty stood, "I think I should go. Let me know what you think of the presentation."

The next morning Shane approached Misty's cubicle with the presentation in hand. He handed it to her. "I've only made a few changes. You were right some of the stuff from the original version was better. I've marked where I want you to return to that version."

She'd expected this, so she'd kept a copy of the original version of the presentation, but she just nodded and took the papers from him.

"Oh, and I'd like the final draft on my desk by lunch time."

"No problem, Shane."

He leaned over her with a smile that didn't match the hard look in his eyes. "Oh, and about what happened in my office. That's just between you and me. Right?"

She nodded. She couldn't afford to lose her job and enraging Shane off was a sure way to make that happen. She and Mitch had been married less than a year and didn't have a spare penny to save.

Misty waited until he walked away, then opened the original file and the second version of the file and started merging the information from the two. She worked without stopping for a break until the new document reflected the latest changes and saved it with yet another name. She wanted a record of every time she changed the presentation just in case she had to answer questions about it.

After she finished making the changes, she left her cubicle. She needed a short walk, a trip to the bathroom, and a cup of coffee. As she was headed back to her desk carrying a full cup of coffee in her favorite ceramic coffee mug with a woman flexing her bicep and the words "Girl Power" in red letters against a black background, she passed Shane in the hallway. He glanced at his watch and smiled. "I hope you're about finished with that presentation."

"It's finished. I just want to read through it once more before I bring it to you."

"Then why are you away from your desk?"

"Seriously, Shane? I needed to use the bathroom and get some coffee."

He looked her up and down. "That blouse is nice. You must be cold. I like it." His gaze lingered on her breasts.

She sighed and took a sip of coffee. "I need to get back to work."

She hurried back to her desk. She didn't dare look back for fear she'd see him watching her walk down the hall, his lust on full display.

She sipped her coffee as she read through the presentation once, twice, thrice. When she couldn't find anything more to change, even slightly, she printed out two copies and headed to Shane's office.

She knocked on his door. "Okay, Shane, here it is. Do you want to discuss it or should I just leave it with you?"

"Come in, we should discuss it. We need to do a practice read through."

She glanced at her watch. "Okay."

They spent the next forty-five minutes reading through the presentation and making notes where to add slides and demonstrations. When it was all done, there were only a few minor tweaks needed to keep them within the thirty minutes they had to do the presentation. They agreed to meet back in his office later that afternoon to do one last read through. Misty left relieved that other than some mild ambiguous flirting most in the form of double entendre, he'd been professional. Maybe he'd gotten the message.

After lunch, Misty sat down at her desk and made all the tweaks to bring the presentation back into their time allotment. When it was done, she turned her attention to some other work she needed to do and kept busy until her meeting with Shane.

At four o'clock, she knocked on his closed door. One of the other girls in the office, whose name she didn't know, opened the door and left looking more than a little flustered. The girl kept her eyes on the ground and walked past Misty so fast there was no time to ask if she was okay.

Misty walked through the door into Shane's office. "What's with…" Misty started to ask but stopped when she saw him sitting behind his desk with his hand in his lap and a devious grin on his face. She felt nauseated as she realized he'd been treating that girl like he treated her. "I have the presentation ready."

He stood and stretched. "Good. Let's get this done."

They went through the presentation again. Everything went smoothly, but Misty thought there were a few changes they could make to tighten it up a bit. Shane said. "You can if you want, but I think it's fine. I need to get out of here. I'm taking my wife out for dinner tonight. Hopefully, I can get her in the mood."

"I hope you have a nice dinner."

"You're so uptight, Misty. You really should chill out. When was the last time you and that husband did it anyway?"

Misty gasped. "Excuse me? That's none of your business, Shane."

"Oh, chill out, Misty."

"Shane, you need to stop this. It's not appropriate."

"Oh, please, Misty. It's all in good fun. I don't mean anything by it. I'm just trying to get to know you. You act like I've committed a crime."

She looked at him and shook her head. "Does your wife know how you act toward other women?"

He laughed. "Are you threatening me?"

"Of course not." She walked toward the door. "But you make me uncomfortable."

He glanced at his watch. "I've got to go. I'll be late. I'll see you tomorrow morning. Be ready to go with this presentation."

Misty approached the table in the restaurant surprised to see only Shane sitting there. "Where's the rest of the team?"

He glanced up from his menu. "This was our project. This is our celebration."

She sat down across from him and looked around. "Oh. I thought everyone was joining us."

He smiled. "I want to talk to you about your future. You have real promise. You showed that in the presentation. Very well done. You impressed everyone in the room."

"Thank you." She picked up her menu. A quick glance showed her exactly what she'd expected. She couldn't afford to eat at the restaurant. She sighed.

"Order whatever you want. It's on me."

"I can't let you do that."

"Oh, not really on me. On the company." He smiled. "After all, we're celebrating. Think of it as a reward for all the money this account will bring in."

"Oh." She smiled and relaxed.

As they ate, she began to wonder if she'd imagined everything that made her feel so uncomfortable about Shane.

They finished lunch, and he paid for both meals. As they left the restaurant, she thanked him again. He smiled and said. "You know, Misty, I'm a good friend to have."

She looked at him not knowing how to respond, so she smiled but said nothing.

"At first I was disappointed you didn't wear the red dress, but this emerald pantsuit might be even better. I noticed how much attention you garnered just walking into the room."

"What?" She looked at him surprised.

He reached over and grabbed her crotch. She backed away bumping into a parking meter. He laughed. "Oh, come on, Misty, you know you want me."

She stumbled backward, her 3-inch heel catching in a crack in the sidewalk. "Damn it, Shane. Enough of this. I'm married. You're married. Leave me alone. It's not going to happen."

He leaned toward her. "Remember what I said about being a good friend to have? Well, I'm a terrible enemy to make. Keep that in mind." He stepped toward her and she backed away again.

His cell phone rang and he pulled it out of his pocket. "Hi Honey, yes, the meeting went fine. I just finished lunch with the team." He turned his back to Misty.

Misty took advantage of the distraction and quickly headed down the street to her car. She was shaking as she sat in the driver's seat catching her breath. She wanted to get out of there before he finished his call.

Back at the office, Misty nodded at the receptionist as she walked past him and down the hall to human resources. This had gone too far. She knocked on the door of the human resources officer, Desra, and entered after being invited in.

She detailed everything that happened to Desra, the human resources officer. Desra listened intently. When she finished, she sat back in her seat. Desra sighed. "Misty, are you sure you want to do this?"

"Excuse me?"

"Look, here's the reality of your situation. You have no proof, and he's not only the director of your department, he's good friends with Donovan."

Misty sat there not knowing what to say. "Are you saying I just have to put up with this treatment?"

"Well, Misty, let's be clear here. We don't condone sexual harassment, but as I said you have no proof. It's your word against his. It's possible you misunderstood, right?" Her expression conveyed the answer she wanted to hear.

"Misunderstood? He grabbed my crotch. I didn't misunderstand that."

Desra sighed. "But you can't prove it."

"What's my recourse?"

"I'll make a note in your file."

"In my file?" She was flabbergasted. "What about his file?"

"You're the one making the report." Desra raised her eyebrows sending a message that made Misty squirm. "We don't want any problems here. My advice is to avoid being alone with him."

Desra returned to the papers on her desk. After a minute she looked up. "Is there something else, Misty?"

"No. I guess not."

Misty went back to her desk fighting back tears. She was angry and disgusted. She picked up some papers and opened a document on her computer. She typed in the numbers from the stack to generate a report until her friend, Gena, stopped by her desk. "How did the presentation go, Misty?"

She looked up. "What?"

"What's wrong?"

Misty couldn't stop her tears. She looked down. "The presentation went fine. I think we'll get the account."

"So then what's wrong?"

"I can't talk about it here."

Gena glanced at her watch. "We're both due for a break. Let's go out and get some fresh air."

They walked outside and took a footpath to a picnic table in a small area behind the building. Misty told Gena what happened from the first time Shane harassed her to telling human resources. Gena listened attentively and nodded a few times.

When Misty finished, Gena looked at her and sighed. "I wondered if he'd gotten to you yet. All the work you've been doing with him."

"What do you mean? He's done this before?"

"Yes, many times. Human resources is well aware. I hate to be the one to tell you this, but they'll probably start trying to make you miserable."

"What do you mean? I've never had a single complaint about my work."

"You will. And, they won't make sense. They'll start pushing you, hoping you'll quit. It's the pattern. The high turnover rate everyone complains about is in large part due to this behavior."

"Desra mentioned his relationship with Donovan."

"Yeah, Donovan does this kind of thing, too, so don't expect anyone to care."

"But Donovan's wife works here."

"Yes, she co-owns the business, and she's very good at pretending it's not happening. She blames the women who work here. She says they're all just trying to start trouble or blackmail them."

Misty looked away. "I can't afford to lose my job."

"I'd suggest you start looking for another one, and in the meantime document everything and never, ever meet with either Donovan or Shane alone."

They headed back into the office. Misty finished out the afternoon without talking to another person at the office. She made sure everything she produced was perfect. When it was time to leave, she left without speaking a word to anyone. She wondered if anyone had noticed her silence.

The next morning she came in to the office to find her inbox overflowing with work and unrealistic deadlines on every item. The work she'd done the day before was marked with questions that were already answered.

Shane stopped by her cubicle a little while later and smiled as he gestured toward her inbox. "Guess you'll be too busy to be complaining now."

She kept quiet and continued typing. He leaned in close. "Make sure you don't make any mistakes. I'd hate to have to fire you."

Over lunch, Misty told Gena about her morning. Gena nodded. "I heard."

"I was hoping it wouldn't come to this. I guess I need to start looking for another job." She paused. "Maybe I should hire a lawyer."

"That's risky."

"You said there are others."

"Yes, there are."

"Maybe I should talk to them. If there's enough, we might have a case."

"It will cost you your job if you decide to go that route."

"I know, but I doubt I'll have a job here much longer anyway. They're setting me up to find grounds to fire me."

"Yes, they are."

A week later, Misty and eleven women who had previously worked at the company met with a lawyer who specialized in sexual harassment cases.

The lawyer listened intently as they each told their stories. She took copious notes and recorded the session as well. She agreed to take their case on contingency.

The women expressed their relief because none of them could afford to hire a lawyer of her caliber, or perhaps any lawyer.

Misty returned to the office after meeting with the lawyer and discovered a message to report to Desra's office.

Desra began speaking before Misty was even seated. "Misty, it's come to our attention that *you're* unhappy here. I need to know if you've discussed our previous meeting with anyone."

"I don't have to answer that."

"That's true. You don't." Desra sat back and sighed. "Look, you've done some good work here and your record reflects that, but your unhappiness here is affecting your job."

"We landed that big account."

"Well. Shane landed that account."

"The presentation he and I created together landed that account."

"His name is the one attached to the account, and he says your contribution was minimal."

"You know better than that."

"It's your word against his."

"Are you firing me?"

"Well, we think it might be best if you resign."

Misty smiled. She'd expected this only it was coming sooner than she expected. "You're asking for my resignation?"

"You'd clearly be happier working elsewhere."

"Yes, I probably would thanks to the hostile working environment here, but I can't afford to just resign."

"See, that's what I mean. You view the environment here as hostile, and that is reflected in your work." Desra smiled. "So are you looking for a new job?"

"I don't have to answer that either."

"No, you don't." She sighed. "I'm not sure we're understanding one another."

"You want me to resign."

"Let's be clear. I didn't actually *ask* for your resignation, but I think we both know this job isn't the best fit for you." Again Desra's expression said what her actual words didn't. "And if your performance reports continue to decline..."

A month later, Misty sat at her kitchen table preparing resumes to mail when her phone rang. Gena spoke quickly and quietly. "Misty, turn on your television."

Misty turned on the television and watched the news report. A reporter stood outside her previous place of work.

The reporter talked about the class action sexual harassment lawsuit that had lead to an investigation of the company. She described a climate of harassment that went far beyond what Misty experienced.

Shane was brought out in handcuffs and the reporter said. "A class action lawsuit against the company for sexual harassment lead to one of the company's directors being charged with rape. He and the owner have also been charged with embezzlement."

Before

Mona's parents often brought her to this beach during her childhood. She couldn't even remember how many summers she spent in the house behind her. That felt like a different lifetime – one she thought of as before. Before her father died. Before her failed marriage. Before her mother's illness. Before all her dreams crashed in front of her face. Before. She and Mama used to sit on the beach watching storms come in until the winds and rain drove pummeled them. Then they ran laughing to the house to be enveloped in huge towels and her father's wonderful comforting bear hugs. She smiled. How she missed those days! Before.

She remembered her father so clearly in spite of the passage of decades. She loved his gruff voice and burly appearance. Her friends felt scared of him at first, even when he had just come home from work dressed in his business suit. He looked like a grizzly bear with his dark hair, sharp almost black eyes, and his six-foot-four husky frame. She smiled. Her friends always ended up laughing at his jokes and wanting to sit on his lap. He was much more like a teddy bear than a grizzly bear. She missed him still.

She showed her mother's day nurse to the door after receiving the daily report that indicated the day had gone much like any other. She went into her room to change quickly. She had gone straight to the beach when she arrived home from work. She hadn't even paused to change out of her plain gray coatdress that did little to accentuate her lack of curves. She had left her pumps and briefcase on the back porch. She needed to bring those in. She still had several accounts to review before bed. Besides she couldn't chance them getting wet from the storm or carried off by a stray dog. Two of her biggest clients weren't happy with the figures she provided them for the previous quarter. Reviewing the figures wouldn't make a big difference, if any, but she would do what she could. She hated accounting. It was so far away from her talents, her pleasure, her dreams.

She slipped on a pair of faded denim shorts, a red t-shirt, and a pair of sandals, and brushed her short dark hair avoiding the mirror. She never liked what she saw there.

She hated looking in her brown eyes because no matter how happy the moment she always saw a hint of sadness, a haunted, longing look for something left behind, a tragic need for something never quite fulfilled. She resolved long ago not to allow bitterness in her life, but the sadness and the longing never seemed to leave.

She walked into the living room. She respected the woman sitting silent and expressionless before the television, but the love she felt for her was in the memories of the strong, spontaneous, creative, caring woman who made up stories to calm her fears, helped her build sand cities on the beach, listened to every problem with an objective mind and a caring heart, stood her ground when she was sure she was right no matter who was offended, had taught her the joy of creating, and had always supported her even when she disagreed with her choices. She closed her eyes and let out a quiet sigh. Mama needed her strength now. That's what she would give her. "Come on, Mama, let's go out to the beach for a few minutes. There's a storm brewing."

Mona watched her mother's pale blue eyes light up. She straightened the older woman's short gray hair with her hand remembering a time when it had flowed down her back in light brown curls. Mama reached for her walker. She could no longer speak, but she had learned to use a walker in the time since her stroke a few years earlier. Mona helped her lift her weaker hand to the walker and watched the proud woman slowly push herself to her feet.

Mona had cared for Mama since her release from the hospital. As an only child, she knew her responsibility and took it seriously.

She paused briefly to set her briefcase and shoes inside as she helped Mama out the door. She slowed her pace to aid her ailing mother down to the beach.

The gathering clouds and accompanying wind cooled the hot summer evening to a welcoming temperature that almost felt like an embrace.

As Mona and Mama stood on the beach and watched the storm clouds roll toward them, Mona smiled as a faint smile spread slowly across Mama's face. Smiling was such an effort that she rarely tried though her eyes always showed her emotions, especially her joy, quite clearly. They stood there, arms linked, until the first few drops of rain started to fall. They couldn't wait until the downpour came like before because Mama couldn't move fast enough to get back to the house.

Mona gently guided her mother toward the house feeling Mama's reluctance to go. Suddenly, the older, thin woman turned back toward the water. One last look. Her blue eyes sparkled with a life Mona hadn't seen since the stroke. Then Mama smiled widely, glanced at her daughter, and turned back to the ocean. Her mouth moved but no sound came out. Mona would later swear she heard her say "I love you, Mona."

A wave crashed loudly as Mama fell to the ground. Mona fell to her knees but knew instantly it was too late as lightning flashed, thunder crashed somewhere in the distance, and the rain began to pelt on her head. "Oh, Mama!"

She half-carried, half-dragged the older woman's thin lifeless body back to the house and carefully placed her on the sofa. She dialed 911 even though her heart screamed there was no point. There was nothing they could do. She sat and held Mama's hand while she waited. Her mother was ready to go. She died happy on the beach, but Mona felt little comfort.

She cried as the paramedics removed the body from the house leaving her instructions on where to go to handle the arrangements. She already knew. She'd been through this before when her father died. Besides the arrangements were already made and paid for. She sat on the sofa and listened to the quiet, her mind a blank canvas.

Then, suddenly, like the lightning flashing outside, it hit her. This was the first time she had been alone in her house for years. She stood and walked into her studio. Finally, she could pursue her dreams. The ones she thought about earlier on the beach. There was nothing to stand in her way. No overbearing, discouraging husband. No ailing mother. Nothing. She could quit her job and paint full time. *Could I really?*

She picked up the paintbrush and started to paint. Slowly at first. She felt momentum building. She wasn't sure what to paint, but she could paint again.

Years ago she almost made her dream a reality. She painted and painted until she created enough good work to have her first gallery showing. She spent weeks deciding which paintings she would show and another week helping arrange the display just right. Then, the night of the opening, she felt crushed when her husband never showed up to see her work on display, to share in her success. He had promised to come straight from there. She looked for him all evening, waiting, desperately wanting to share her success with him.

That night she sold ten of her paintings. The gallery owner told her it was the most she'd ever sold at a new artist's first showing. She excitedly bounced into her house, this house, deciding to just forget he never arrived at the gallery. She found her husband sitting behind his desk in a rage. "Mona, you will stop this art nonsense and get a job. It's time you pulled your weight around here. We could be so much better off if you worried more about our future together and less about this art shit."

"What the hell are you talking about?"

"I'm the only one around here keeping us afloat. I'm tired of it. How the hell did you pay for that damn dress? I'll tell you how. My money."

He'd apparently forgotten he was living in *her* house and that she'd used the trust her father set up for her to pay off his student loans.

"But I sold ten of my paintings tonight."

"Big deal. Get a job or you're on your own."

"Fine, get the hell out of my house. My father left me this house when he died. Get out. Do you really think I need your support? I'm sick of this fight with you."

He left in a huff with a single suitcase. She was sure he thought she would beg him to come back. It never happened. She actually felt a strange sense of relief that he was gone.

A month later when she wrote him a check to cover the percentage of the earnings from the ten paintings the divorce settlement stated she owed him, he gasped. Then he started begging her to take him back. She laughed in his face. "Bet you wish you waited to see how much I made from that showing, don't you?"

Mona walked away from him and never looked back. His own stupidity and rashness had gotten him where he was, and she no longer cared.

She had made a few bad investments and lost some of the money. She sold five more paintings in the months following her gallery opening. She kept painting. She booked a few more shows and did a couple of consignment jobs.

Several months after her divorce, her mother had a stroke. She possessed neither the time nor the energy to pain while her mother was convalescing, well as much as she would ever recover. Gallery openings were completely out of the question. Over the next year, the medical bills almost depleted her remaining money.

She couldn't bear the thought of Mama in a nursing home, so she brought her home with her and hired a nurse. As her funds fell lower and lower and her painting time grew ever scarcer, she was forced to start looking for another source of income. She finally took a position with a local accounting firm. Between her job and caring for her mother, she had little time or energy left for her art. Over time, she learned to live with it, but she never felt happy.

Now, suddenly, all that had changed. She would work days, paint nights, do her next show within a year and quit her job. She formulated the plan while she painted. She needed to get back in touch with her old art circle, and see what was happening. She needed to visit some galleries and talk to their owners. She should pull some of her old work out, dust it off, and try to do a show sooner. Then she could stage a grand comeback once her name was recognizable in the art world again. There was so much to do, so much to plan.

She stepped back from her painting pleased with the effect. One side of the canvas showed the sun beating down on the ocean waves and the beach. The other side showed the storm clouds and the darkening sky closing in over waves growing harsher and angrier. With her brush, she muted the dividing line bringing the storm over the edge of the sunny side. It was perfect.

She skipped supper. She signed the painting in the lower right corner and set it aside to dry. Then she went to the kitchen, fixed a sandwich, and returned to her studio. The sun was just coming up as she placed a fresh canvas on her easel.

The doorbell rang. She answered the door with her paintbrush in her hand, painting dripping on her jeans. Mama's nurse stood on the porch. She told her her services would no longer be needed and why, thanked her for her hard world and promised her a great reference letter. As the nurse offered her condolences, she nodded but said nothing. The nurse turned to leave and she closed the door wondering why the nurse had looked at her so strangely. Then she shrugged and headed back to her studio.

A dam holding her creativity had broken. She couldn't stop painting. Some of the work was terrible, some needed a lot of work, some a little touching up, and some was perfect. But none of that mattered. All that mattered was she was painting again. She felt alive for the first time since her mother's stroke.

She painted, holding a sandwich in one hand and a paintbrush in the other rather than stop to eat. Nothing would ever stand in the way of her dreams, her goals again. She wouldn't let it.

Exhausted, she fell back on the couch in her studio. She had worked for more than twenty-four hours straight, and she had no energy. She would handle the difficult things tomorrow. She was probably out of a job, but, then again, people reacted strangely to grief, so she might be okay. She closed her eyes sure she should feel guilty about her zeal.

She should be grieving her mother's death. She didn't recognize the feeling in her soul, but it wasn't grief. Mama suffered for so long, and she looked so at peace when she died that Mona struggled to feel sad. Her mother hadn't been Mama since the stroke, and she had been unhappy even though she had been unable to express it with words.

Mona looked around the room. She wondered what she should do. She needed to go to the funeral home. She needed to call her aunts and her uncle. She needed to call work. She wondered if she should call the nurse and apologize for being so abrupt. She just wanted to paint.

With the phone calls to her mother's siblings made, she fell into a fitful sleep. They had taken the news well. The consensus seemed to be that all were relieved her suffering had ended. They all expressed sentiments that indicated they had also mourned Mama after the stroke.

She rushed through her morning chores with her thoughts on her canvas and her fingers itching to wrap around a brush. She took bereavement time, as much as the firm allowed, and a few vacation days as well.

With the plans all settled, she rushed back to her studio and started to paint again. She loved the feel of the brush in her hand, the paint splattering on her clothes. She looked down. She still wore the simple black dress she had worn to the funeral home to make the arrangements. It was paint stained now, but she didn't care. She ran the brush down the front leaving a stroke of yellow paint. She shrugged. The stripe of yellow paint improved the appearance of the ridiculously overpriced dress.

She kicked off her pumps hearing them plop against the wall and continued painting. This time as her inspiration guided her, she painted an abstract portrait of her parents in the clouds. They looked like they had... Before....

She stepped back to see it from a distance. A small tear slid down her cheek. Her parents approved of her choice to live life on her own terms. She felt it in the depths of her soul. She loved them and they her. That kind of love could never be taken from her memories, her heart, her life. She would always feel their presence, their influence, and all the wonderful lessons they taught her. The lived on in her heart and in the woman she had become. She smiled.

She was determined to make art her career, her life, her legacy. She didn't care if she had to go hungry, if she had to live penniless, if it took the rest of her life, she would bring her work back to the public, back to the world, back to life. She looked at the faces on the canvas, and she saw not the old man or the ailing old woman they had become, but the youthful, energetic, caring parents they had been. She recognized the *before* in the painting. She smiled.

She'd found her passion again. There was the evidence of it all around her. Her creativity, her life, her dreams, freedom...

Before...

After...

Grandma's Table

Tamile looked at the heavy, solid wood table full of food. For as long as she could remember, Grandma had shown her love by cooking all the family member's favorite dishes at family gatherings. Tamile learned at an early age how a simple compliment made a dish forever a favorite. She forced what she hoped passed for a genuine smile in contrast to Grandma's open, beaming face.

Some food tasted okay, but it all felt so gross in her mouth. She hated the textures of food – all food. Maybe she should tell Grandma how repulsed she felt by the heavily laden table, but she dismissed the idea as quickly as it hit her mind. Grandma wouldn't understand. Her true feelings about food would be equivalent to rejecting Grandma's love. She could never do that. She loved Grandma way too much to hurt her like that.

Tamile looked at the southern feast and shook her head. Another large family meal to get through. *Why did everything have to revolve around food?*

The excess disgusted her. She struggled to keep her face cheerful lest her distaste become apparent to all. She stared at a huge roast surrounded by carrots and potatoes, a platter of fried chicken, another filled with fried fish, and yet another displaying baked pork chops. She almost gagged looking at all that meat. She turned her gaze to macaroni cooked in tomato juice, macaroni and cheese, homemade biscuits, and white bread. Green beans with a piece of bacon peeking through, potatoes slightly yellow from the butter in which they had been boiled, mashed potatoes, peas, tomatoes, and a large bowl of cucumbers in vinegar were spread throughout the table. Lastly, she saw the jars of pickles, pickled beets, jellies – all homemade, and a small plate with a huge slab of softening butter.

As she hugged Grandma, she looked over her shoulder to the buffet table against the wall. She almost groaned aloud at the display. In the center of the table was a huge two-layer round chocolate cake with chocolate frosting. A lemon pie and a pumpkin pie set on the left of the cake and on its right a chocolate pie and a pecan pie. One end of the table held a bowl of fruit salad. On the other end a Jell-O salad jiggled as her uncle bumped into the buffet table.

Every family dinner at her grandparents' house focused entirely too much on food in Tamile's opinion. Maybe this really wasn't so much food when you needed to feed eight children all with spouses and so many grandchildren Tamile had lost count. Still just looking at it disgusted her. She always dreaded that moment when one of her uncles said, "Let's eat!" and rubbed his hands together.

She smiled as Grandma pointed to the chocolate cake and the roast beef indicating she'd fixed Tamile's favorites. Maybe when she was ten, and that had been more than ten years ago. Then again, she never really liked them all that much then either. Cake had that moist texture that no matter how hard she tried she just couldn't get out of her mouth. And roast, oh, God, roast. Roast took forever to chew keeping it in her mouth way too long. Tamile held her silence. Suddenly she felt ill.

As soon as Grandma turned to greet the next slew of grandchildren arriving, Tamile slipped off to find a quiet corner. She wanted nothing more than to forget about all that food. Food she would have to eat, or at least pretend to eat. Over the years she had learned to pretend very well. Take small portions, eat tiny bites that she could barely detect, chatter nonstop if someone came near, discretely dump the rest of the food in the trash as soon as possible without detection and swear she was full. She could do it. She'd done it a million times.

No matter what food she ate, chewy or crunchy, moist or dry, mushy or hard, she couldn't stand to have the stuff in her mouth.

She longed for the day when food would no longer be necessary.

She imagined ways to nourish her body without food. She imagined injecting the necessary nourishment directly into the stomach, thought of ways to combine all of life's food necessities into liquid form. She envisioned a life where food just became unnecessary, where the body could get its fuel from the air itself. Maybe someday someone would invent a pill that would fill her stomach and provide all the nutrition she needed. A pill she wouldn't have to feel in her mouth. One that would just slide down her throat and expand to a filling, nutritious meal once it hit her stomach. She sighed while she day-dreamed solutions to avoid food. She dreaded getting through yet another family meal.

She watched her family *ooh* and *ah* over the table, and she wondered if any of them shared her feelings about food. She didn't think so. They relished their food, taking huge bites, savoring the various tastes in their mouths, taking their time chewing, and always cleaning their plates. She hated to watch them eat. She hated for anyone to see her eat. *How could anyone enjoy doing something so disgusting?*

She preferred eating alone. Then she could read or watch television or do anything to block out the food going into her mouth. She could almost forget she was eating long enough to nourish her body – healthy food in small portions. She didn't worry about getting fat. That had never been an issue for her. She understood why she needed food, she just couldn't bring herself to enjoy it. She tried because she was supposed to, but she just couldn't.

She watched her family line up to fill their plates. Thank goodness she wouldn't have to sit at the table. She could more easily eat less and dispose of the rest when she didn't have watchful eyes on her. She got in line and put a little of almost everything on her plate except the meat, and of that she took only a very small slice of the roast. She stood back and looked at the table full of food once more. Then she looked around the kitchen, the living room, and out into the yard where her family had scattered to eat. They laughed and joked, shared the food from their plates with each other, and gobbled down as much as they could as fast as possible. No one struggled with food. She sighed and carried her plate out the door and over to a secluded tree, so no one witnessed her struggle with each bite or saw how much she threw away.

She stared at her still half-full plate. She jumped when a hand squeezed her shoulder. She set her plate on the ground. An arm slipped around her shoulders. She looked up. "Tamile, my darling granddaughter, it's a pretty awful thing to do, isn't it?" Grandma nodded toward her plate.

She tried to remember the last time she'd seen Grandma eat at one of these large, family dinners. Grandma kissed her forehead, turned, walked back to the house. *A kindred spirit, perhaps?*

The Letter

To Whomever:

When I woke up this morning I couldn't think of five good reasons to get out of bed. I stared at the ceiling and debated what right I had to take up space on the earth. I've let down everyone who's ever cared about me – including, no especially, myself.

Finally, I pulled myself out of bed and started my day - a day like most of the other days of my life. I went through the motions just as expected. The whole time I tried to come up with five good reasons I deserve to live. Too bad none ever came to me – not legitimate ones anyway.

I thought back over my life and wondered where it all went wrong. I thought I was on the right track for so long. It's only now I realize it was never *my* track. But now it's too late.

All of it seems so pointless now. I tried to do it all right, to be the perfect daughter, perfect sister, perfect student, the perfect friend, the perfect lawyer. I tried to make everyone happy, but I failed miserably.

I still remember the first time I felt like I wasn't perfect enough. I was either six or seven. I was helping Mom plant flowers in front of the house. I remember they were pretty – all different colors like a rainbow. I felt so proud of the group I planted until I saw Mom digging them up and moving them into a *better* arrangement. Hearing Mom's mumbling about the time it was taking her to redo them stayed with me. It would play over in my head whenever I tried to do anything. I didn't want to be the reason Mom needed to do extra work.

The first time I brought home a B on my report card, the disappointment on Dad's face made me cry even before he grounded me for a week. I think I was in second grade then. I worked hard never to make less than an A again. That often wasn't enough either. I remember being asked why an A wasn't an A+. I think it was his way of pushing me to do my best, but by that point I didn't need pushing. Finally, the pressure got to me and all my grades slipped to Bs and even a C. I felt so guilty I worked twice as hard to do better and quickly returned to achieving almost all 'As'. I struggled so hard but could never quite keep them there. There was always one class or the other that gave me trouble. Usually the one in which I couldn't muster any interest.

I tried so hard to be as perfect as I could, to be what everyone wanted me to be. I'm so worn out I don't think I can do it anymore. I'm not sure what striving for all that perfection even got me. Did it make all those people I was trying to please happy? I don't think so. It certainly never brought me any joy.

I don't blame anyone else. This was my own doing. If I'd lived my life better, I'd be loved. I'd be happy. I should've known better. I tried to do it right.

During my high school years, I practically stopped eating. I never thought I was fat. I didn't particularly like food. I didn't like going to the bathroom. I couldn't stand to watch people eat, and I didn't want to do anything that would make me look like that. The process of eating grossed me out. Besides it was just so time consuming. It was just a plus that eating that little kept me slim. I was careful to eat enough to keep myself active and alert. After all, I soon discovered that without some food, I became drowsy and developed trouble concentrating. That affected my grades negatively, and I couldn't let that happen.

I played by the rules even after I moved into a residence hall when I started college. At first I went home every weekend to make Mom and Dad happy not to mention my high school friends – the few that I had. When I went home, I spent more and more time with Mom and Dad because they got so disappointed whenever I went out with friends. Soon though taking the maximum class load, I found it necessary to stay on campus and use my weekends for homework. After all, perfect grades took work.

I tried never to ask for more than I needed to survive from anyone especially my parents. I called every week as expected. I listened to my friends' problems even if it meant getting up at three in the morning for them or staying up all night to finish homework they interrupted.

I learned, after a couple of drunken nights out with friends, to trick them by sipping one drink all evening and pretending to be wasted as the night progressed-- especially if I had to finish homework when I got back to my room. I tried to never burden anyone. I don't think I succeeded with that. But I got good grades, took care of my friends, met the man of my parents' dreams (who dumped me because "You're just wound too tight for me."), held down a part-time job, and graduated with honors.

Law school, or should I say stress school, left me struggling daily – hell, hourly – to disguise how frazzled I felt. My social life became extinct as I struggled to keep my grades perfect. Between homework, making Law Review, and my part-time job I existed on about four hours of sleep a night for almost three years. Still, I managed to visit Mom and Dad every time they asked or I anticipated they were about to ask. I never told them how miserable I felt. Not even when I broke up with the man of my dreams because, despite his protests, I just couldn't be the perfect girlfriend that he deserved, and I certainly couldn't afford to entertain the idea of trying to be the perfect wife. He tried for a while to change my mind, but even the best man can be driven away with a concerted effort. Besides, even though I loved him, Mom and Dad hated him. I refused to disappoint them no matter how happy I felt with him. My time with him tempted me to relax and enjoy life. I had no time for that.

From time to time, I still suffer from the "what if" syndrome when I think about that perfect man. Somewhere deep inside I think I've been holding on to the romance-book notion that someday, somewhere, we'd run into each other again. I'd be able to be perfect for him and our love would pick up right where it left off. Then I'd finally be able to break free of my drive for perfection, of my need to be all to all.

I turned my back on him all those years ago though, and I lost touch with him. I hope he found the happiness he so deserved. I so wished, and still wish, I knew how to give him everything he deserved.

Even before I graduated from law school, top law firms from all over the United States courted me. I wanted to go to work for the district attorney's office, but Dad said I should take the position in San Francisco. I took his advice and moved across the country for the position. My trips back east grew ever less frequent over the next couple of years as I worked hard to advance at the firm. Still, I figured out a way to make time to be available for every family event possible. Guilt ate away at my heart and soul every time I had to miss an event because of work. Yet Mom and Dad wanted my success so much that I felt torn between what I knew it would take to get to the level to finally make them proud of me and the disappointment in me they expressed every time I couldn't be there for an event. I never told them how I felt, and I don't remember being asked.

Did anyone ever care how I felt? Did anyone ever care what I wanted? Did anyone ever care if I was happy? Did I even care? How could I expect anyone else to care when I'm not even sure if I ever did?

When I made junior partner at the firm I felt so happy. I thought Dad and Mom would finally be proud of me. Instead, Dad asked, "So what's next? A senior partnership? Or politics maybe?"

Mom said, "Well, at least you've got that. I guess that means we'll see even less of you."

Suddenly my happiness evaporated. I was right back where I'd always been. Trying my best to be what everyone wanted, thinking I'd achieved it, and learning I failed again. I still didn't quite measure up.

A few weeks ago two options became available – a senior partnership with the firm and a judgeship. Now I'm faced with making a decision when I'm not sure I want either. I called Dad to get his opinion and he was no help. He told me it was time for me to make my own decisions. I'm terrified of disappointing him when I finally make a decision. Mom just wanted to know when I'm coming for a visit. The biggest problem is I don't want any of it. I don't even want to get up in the morning. I want to take all the money in my accounts and run off to some island. In my fantasy, the man of my dreams walks up to me on the beach and recognizes me immediately. He tells me he's waited all these years for me and we open a little bar where there's always laughter and music.

But that's the fantasy....

Reality proves that fantasy can never come true. I didn't even know how much I relied on that fantasy until three days ago. I sat on my sofa, sipped a glass of wine, and thumbed through the alumni magazine from law school when there he was. I stopped at the photo. He was as handsome as ever. My eyes finally left his face and saw the words beside it. It took a moment for it to register with me that he was dead. Reading the first few lines told me all I needed to know. He died in a sailing accident while on vacation in the Caribbean. And with those words, my fantasy died.

Now, I know how much I've wasted my life. I've never lived it for me. Here I am a successful corporate lawyer on the cusp of choosing between two very respected top positions in my field with enough money to retire whenever I want, and all I can think about is that I have no idea who I am or what I want out of life. My only vacations are for trips to visit my parents. I take care of the people around me, but I wouldn't call any of them friends. Turning to someone with my problems would be a sign of weakness, so I keep them inside. Losing my fantasy depressed me more than when I broke up with him all those years ago.

What would happen if I walked away from it all? What would happen if I just made myself happy? What would happen if I stopped worrying about what everyone else wants from me?

I can't disappoint. I can't live knowing I'm the reason for my parents' disappointment. How can I choose between the two job offers? No matter what I choose someone will be disappointed. And, I'm not even sure what I want. I just don't want to have to decide. I can't decide. I'm too exhausted to think about it anymore.

How can I ever be happy? I know that if I do what makes me happy, I'll make everyone else unhappy. I'll let everyone down. I can't be responsible for that. I don't deserve happiness at everyone else's expense.

I can't take this anymore. My head hurts, my stomach hurts, and I just wish I could sleep forever. I wish I didn't have to think about anything. I wish I thought things could be different. I wish I managed to think of five reasons to wake up tomorrow. This just can't be how life is supposed to be. I just can't live with myself anymore. I just can't take this confusion anymore. I feel like I'm going to explode. I'm sorry everyone.

I'm so sorry.

Love always,

Me

The Broken Dock

Rayanne grabbed the printout of her speech and slipped out of her hotel room wearing her sunglasses and a floppy straw hat with a blue and white ribbon around it. She smoothed down the front of her sundress smiling at the abstract white magnolias on the blue background. Her blue sandals completed the look and weren't exactly practical for the walk, but they were so much cuter than her sneakers.

She walked the mile to the pond where she'd spent so much time during her college years. She hadn't been back here in years – had thought she'd never return. Life had taken her in a different direction, and she never looked back - never wanted to look back. Too much bad stuff lived under that particular dock. Peeking into the dark water underneath was far too dangerous.

But then…

She'd gotten the invitation to give a speech on campus. So here she was. As she prepared to return to campus, she became excited about sitting on the dock again. She rounded the pond and the dock came into view.

Ducks still skimmed the surface. The trees still swayed in the wind. The surface still rippled. The grass was neatly cut. She stepped around the duck poop with a smile. Even though she knew she shouldn't, she pulled a couple of slices of bread from her pocket and fed the ducks and fish. She stopped suddenly as the heavy chain came into view, the heavy chain that prevented her from using the metal ladder to descend to the dock.

She stepped closer to the dock and blinked back a tear as she looked down. The dock mirrored her shattered and splintered memories. She looked down at the rusted bolts and buoys, the rotted wood covered with growing moss, and the holes. She stared into the water underneath the dock as it splashed into the voids left by the missing planks.

She stepped over the chain and climbed down anyway. She carefully placed her feet on a steady looking plank that showed the least amount of visible rot. She envisioned the dock as whole as it was all those years ago when she sat here writing speeches for her classes, researching papers, and studying. She remembered coming to the dock to find peace from the drama of broken relationships and the chaos of her life then.

She'd sworn when she left this place she'd never return. There were too many memories that splintered her heart and created chaos in her mind. She stood and looked down at the peaceful water thinking of all the times she'd come here to escape.

Somehow over the years even with her splintered memories and broken heart, she'd pieced herself back together in a way the dock that used to be whole could never do. She stood on the dock and felt it sway lightly under her feet and thought of all that had happened. She opened the papers in her hand, determined to read them sitting on this dock just like she'd done so many times in those earlier days. Finding no place secure enough to sit, she balanced on the broken boards and began to read the words feeling their instability matching the wobble of the broken dock. She couldn't give this speech. This speech didn't reflect the whole truth. She'd prettied it up. She'd written it to impress, not her audience but some imaginary professor who wouldn't be grading her.

The university had invited her to speak about her research into sexual assault and sexual harassment and the organization she'd created to combat both yet her speech read like a dry term paper. She stared out over the water thinking of every time she'd taken inspiration from the depths of the pond.

"Ma'am." She heard a voice behind her and turned to see a familiar face. She wondered if he recognized her.

She smiled but didn't betray that she recognized him as she

said. "Yes?"

"You're not supposed to be on that dock. It isn't safe."

"I'm a grown woman. I can decide for myself."

"Damn, Rayanne, I thought that was you." He offered her his hand, but she didn't move. "Come on now."

"Nope, Conner." She smiled at him. "I'm going to stay here a little while longer."

He sighed. "I haven't seen you in… How long has it been?"

"About 10 years give or take a few months."

"Come on up from there before you fall in."

"Still trying to save me from myself, Conner?" She laughed. "Don't you ever learn?"

He looked at her. "I could call campus security."

"But you won't and we both know it."

"That dock isn't safe. That's why they have it blocked off."

"Yeah, with a chain anyone can just step right over. Please."

"What are you doing here anyway?"

"I'm giving a speech on campus tonight."

"Really?"

"Yes, really. Why are you here?"

"I teach on campus. I tend to walk around campus after my last class of day and stop by here most days."

"Wow! I never would've guessed you'd end up teaching here." She looked around. "Honestly, I thought you'd be like me and get the hell out of here and never come back."

He laughed. "So did I."

She looked out over the water and then down at the papers in her hand. She sighed.

"Rayanne, let me buy you cup of coffee. We can catch up."

This time she laughed. "So now you're resorting to bribery to get me off this dock."

"Well, if that's what it takes. That dock is broken and dangerous."

"Yeah, I know. Something should be done about that. It should be here for other students to enjoy the way I did." She turned and took hold of the rails of the ladder. Conner reached out his hand to take her other one. She forgot about the papers in her hand as she reached forward and loosened her grip. They went flying, the fast majority landing in the pond. "Damn. There goes my speech."

"I'm so sorry, Rayanne." He scrambled to gather the papers that weren't in the water.

"Don't worry about it. It sucked anyway. I need to totally rewrite it."

He picked up a page and looked at it. "What is this?"

"My speech."

"Why would you put yourself through this?"

"What?"

"After what happened to you… Why?"

"This is what I do, Conner."

"What do you mean this is what you do?"

"I started this organization. I research sexual assault, sexual harassment, and violence against women in general."

He looked almost angry. "I don't understand. What happened to you almost destroyed you. Why would you make it your life's work?"

"Because it almost destroyed me. Because it me as broken as this dock. Because I had to find a way to use my experience for something good. Because I had to stop hiding…" She looked down at the dock and then back at his face. "Do you want to forget about the coffee?"

"What?" He looked around. "No, of course not. Why would I? Let's go."

"Look, if it's too much, I understand."

"It's not that." He handed her the papers. "It's that I always pictured you off somewhere happily married with a house full of kids with all this behind you, barely a splinter in your life."

"Yeah, it doesn't work like that, Conner."

"I know but I wanted it to…for you."

"I have a good life. I love what I do."

He pointed in what she assumed was the direction of a coffee shop as they walked. She followed his lead. They walked in silence for awhile. Campus was still beautiful, but places she'd loved were replaced by new buildings or parking lots or grassy quads.

Once they ordered coffee and were seated outside in a garden, she looked at him. "What about you? Are you happy?"

"Yeah, I am. Teaching suits me."

"That's good."

"So what about you? Got a husband and house full of kids

waiting for you?

She laughed. "I never married and have no kids. I've had a series of somewhat serious relationships, but I value my independence far too much to get married. And I never, ever wanted kids. I don't even have pets. I travel far too much. You?"

"I married once. It was short lived. No kids though she did miscarry once, so early in the pregnancy it didn't even feel real yet. Since then, I've had a couple of serious relationships."

"I always thought you'd be the white picket fence family man type."

"So did I, but apparently not."

They sat in silence for several long minutes. Birds chirped nearby. Water bubbled in water fountains. The wind blew the flowers to and fro. They sipped their coffee, each lost in thought.

Finally, Conner broke the silence. "Why did you say your speech sucked?"

"Because it did."

"That's not an answer."

She sighed. "Because it lacked connection. Because it lacked the personal story that would bring it to life. Because it was written like I was trying to impress a professor. Because I wrote it like I wanted to please the university instead of telling the full truth about my experience."

"I doubt it was as bad as you think."

"Oh, it was. It was a departure from the speech I usually give. But I've never given it at the scene of the crime, so to speak." She downed the last of her coffee. "Walk with me?"

"Where?"

"To the scene of the crime."

"What?"

"I want to go there. I want to return to the scene of the crime."

"I don't think that's a good idea."

She stood up and held her head high. "I'm going. You can come with me or not, but I'm going."

She didn't look back to see if he followed her. As she got closer to the spot, her breath grew shallow and her chest felt tight. She looked at the windows. The sun glinted off them. She stopped. She felt the memories wash over her as she stared at the window of the room where her life had been ripped from her and she'd been forced onto a path she never wanted to travel.

She closed her eyes. She felt Conner standing behind her. He didn't touch her. He was too smart for that. Or perhaps he just feared her reaction. There was the before and the after of who she was and who she became wrapped up in the moments that occurred in that room.

She opened her eyes and turned to Conner. "I need to go now. I know what my speech needs to say. Can you drive me back to my hotel?"

"Sure."

An hour later she sat on the wall beside the broken dock with her laptop on her lap and wrote the first lines of the speech that finally, finally spoke her full, unadulterated broken truth.

The next evening as she spoke the words to a room full of college students, professors, and administrative staff including her dear friend, Conner, she stood in her vulnerability and her power.

"Yesterday I came to campus with a speech in hand. That speech is now floating beneath the broken dock that mirrors my experience on this campus so many of you currently call home. See, right here on this very campus my life splintered into two parts just like the planks of that dock. The girl I was before I was raped and the girl I was after I was raped. They resembled each other, but I was forever changed in ways that left me with holes that might never be repaired. To that end, I made it my life's mission to find a way to help other girls not have to be the before girl and the after girl who sees herself reflected in a broken dock..."

Nothingness

Marianna leaned her head back against the headboard and smiled. She listened to the rain beat against the window. She ran away from home four days earlier. She left a note on the kitchen table and left. Maybe a thirty-seven year old woman should call her exodus something else, but the label fit.

She stood and stretched. Maybe Napa Valley hadn't been her best choice for an escape from her life. The rain started as she drove into town. She'd come here because her last visit was so full of joy. She wanted to recapture joy or at least remind herself what it felt like. She wanted to convince herself to return to the life she used to love. Only recently life felt so pointless.

One morning she awoke unable to see the point in her job or in anything else either. She stared at her ceiling and wondered what difference trying to make a difference accomplished. The world had been trying to solve the same problems in varying forms as long as there had been a world - poverty, famine, racism, family issues... No one ever solved problems only managed them until the next generation took over the effort.

The same wars had been fought over and over since the beginning of time. Sure the leaders names changed and the weapons became more deadly and less personal. If one studied history it soon became clear that no war ever really ended anything. It only postponed the issue until someone else from a new generation awakened it from a new angle but with the same results – death and destruction.

She tried to talk to her husband, John, about what she felt, but he only stared at her blankly. As a scientist, he liked things to line up in neat little facts that weren't open to a million different emotional responses and interpretations. Her work as a family therapist required her to make a difference in the lives of the families she treated. If she couldn't see the point, she couldn't do her job. She arranged for her partner, Jamie, to take over her cases for a while, and she went home unsure what to do with herself. She thought that a few days off would snap her out of it, but it hadn't. That's when she ran away.

She even struggled to see the point of relationships – friendships, co-workers, even her marriage – all seemed pointless to her at the moment because she couldn't see what they meant for the long term. It wasn't that she wanted to end her relationships. Not at all. She loved John. She loved her son. She loved her friends. She cared about her co-workers. Somewhere deep down the feelings still existed. She didn't want to hurt anyone. She just couldn't see the purpose of any of it.

People had been trying to get all these things right since the beginning of civilization. It wasn't like a movie where at the end all the issues were resolved. No, the problems of the world never really changed. Happily ever after didn't exist. Movies and books really caused people to set their expectations for happy endings way too high. The only real ending was death.

Marianna left her room. People sat in the living room of the bed and breakfast and discussed friendly activities. No one seemed all that excited about touring vineyards in the rain. She hesitated for a moment tempted to tell them that after a couple of wine tastings, they would no longer care about the rain or the tours. They probably already knew that. So what if they got a little muddy? It's not like anyone would know or care in a hundred years. Hell, they wouldn't even care by tomorrow. Same applied to her opinion, so she slipped out the front door and dashed to her car.

She settled behind the steering wheel, brushed her wet hair back from her forehead, started the car, and stared out at the rain for a few minutes. She didn't know where she wanted to go, but she needed to get out of that room. Even the idea of pointless chatter irritated her. She glanced at her cell phone to verify it was fully charged. She felt a little surprised – and hurt, if she admitted the truth to herself – that John hadn't called yet. Either he felt really angry or he understood she needed some time to get a grip on things. Her guess was the first. Maybe he just didn't care, but she refused to believe that.

She slipped the phone into the cup holder on the passenger side. She pulled out of the parking lot and drove toward San Francisco. Even through the rain, the vineyards looked beautiful. They didn't do much for her state of mind at the moment though. They served as just one more thing man exploited in the name of advancing the world. Wine tasted delicious, but what was the point really? Would it make the world a better place or just line the pockets of the owners? What the hell difference did it make? All the people who worked the ground would eventually die just like the owners of the companies who owned the vineyards. What did wealth do besides possibly prolong the inevitable?

She drove aimlessly turning from one road to another without a destination in mind. She didn't even care. She just wanted to keep moving.

No loss or trauma precipitated the development of nothingness she felt. Her life had been completely normal when she awoke with this painful numbness. She tried to explain it. She tried to reason it away. She tried to move through it. She tried to behave her way out of it.

Marianna listened to the anguish in an abused wife's voice as she talked about initiating divorce proceedings against her abuser and her children's reactions. Another woman described her best friend holding her down and raping her because she "needed to learn to enjoy sex again." A man cried for half an hour because he was consumed with grief over his wife's death after a long illness. A teenager described years of sexual abuse by her grandfather and her father. The whole time they talked, Marianna's thoughts repeatedly returned to the idea they all faced the same fate. So would she. Death loomed before them all.

She needed to make a change. If she continued to treat these people in her current state of mind, she'd do them more harm than good. At least she'd been able to see that and leave before she hurt anyone. At first she'd thought she suffered from burnout. It made sense. She'd listened to these same problems from different faces for more than ten years professionally and for as long as she could remember on a personal level. After a while, the anguished faces started to take on certain similarities. A deadness settled in the traumatized eyes. She recognized that look not only in her patient's eyes but also in the eyes of friends, family, people she'd just met and even strangers on the street. When she'd looked in the mirror one morning and recognized that deadness in her own eyes, she looked away opting to ignore it until she no longer could. She hid it from everyone including her partner and her husband.

Marianna noticed the coast before her. She parked and exited the car. She walked down to the deserted beach. She breathed in the rain soaked salty air and longed to feel excited about life. She stood at the edge of the surf and stared out over the choppy water. The dark gray clouds hung low in the sky, but the rain had paused.

She no longer even felt anger at the injustices in the world. Her motivation to make the world a better place disappeared with that anger. No matter what she did, no matter what anyone did, it wouldn't change anything. When she started her career, she promised herself she would refuse to allow that kind of bitterness to invade her life. But she didn't feel bitterness, she felt – dare she admit it – defeated.

Even all those people in the history books and whose names were attached to scientific discovery hadn't really changed the world. The world still struggled along with its issues. All those contributions and poverty still existed. Murder still occurred far too often. Rape remained rampant. Abuses of human rights happened without relenting. Illness still took lives. Wars over religion, land, money, and ultimately power never stopped. The daily atrocities never really changed.

Large droplets of rain fell on her head as she walked back to her car. She stopped and turned toward the water. She could walk out into the surf and it wouldn't make a difference – not really.

As she drove back toward the bed and breakfast, she glanced in the rearview mirror. The sun sank far out on the horizon behind her. Another day disappeared with her lost in a void of nothingness. Her stomach rumbled. She looked at her watch. She looked around but found no place to eat. Vineyards and fields surrounded her. She recognized no landmarks. She hoped the road lead back to the bed and breakfast. A little voice in her head reminded her she might be lost and should feel anxious about being alone in the middle of nowhere, but she felt nothing.

Nothingness felt worse than anything she remembered. Even the rage that consumed her as a teenager seemed preferable to nothingness. Of course, she preferred the optimism she'd felt as a new college graduate. Even the despair she felt after the miscarriage of her first child felt better than this nothingness. She thought back over her life and realized that at various times she'd felt every known emotion and at times many at once.

She watched as a bolt of lightning lit up the sky.

The consuming nature of nothingness surprised her. It smothered her, smashed her, and ripped her apart all at the same time.

As she rounded a curve a small café suddenly popped into view. She turned into the parking lot without signaling. The car behind her blew its horn, a long, angry wail ripped through the quiet night. She glanced in the rearview mirror and shrugged. She felt no guilt, unusual for her, that her actions inconvenienced someone else.

She chose a table near a dark window, ordered a cup of coffee, and stared out at the rain creating paths down the window pane. She watched a series of rain drops run together creating a web. Nothingness trapped her like the prey in a spider's web. No matter which way she turned, no matter how hard she struggled, no matter how she tried to free herself she felt more entangled.

She wrapped her hands around the cup of hot coffee the waitress set in front of her. She let the warmth penetrate her finger for a few minutes before sipping the weak, watery coffee.

A few minutes later the waitress set the sandwich and soup Marianna ordered in front of her. She barely acknowledged the waitress with a quick nod because she was focused on the web of water that streamed down the window pane. She slowly ate her sandwich one deliberate bite at a time.

Noises drifted toward her, but she heard them as if through a bubble. She heard muted sounds of laughter. Families discussed their day. A group of businessmen chatted amicably about a meeting. A cell phone rang and she heard one of the businessmen leave his table and ask someone - she assumed his child - about school before saying good night. Another cell phone rang and she heard a man promise to call "hon" as soon as he got back to his room. A woman scolded her small son who apparently was more interested in exploring the restaurant than eating his dinner.

She tried to see a point to the activity of those around her, but she found it all so pointless. Regardless of what all these people achieved, their lives faced the same end as everyone else's. They could be as polite as they wanted, as strict on their children, as loving family men and as strong deal makers as they wanted to be and it wouldn't make any difference in the end. She finished her dinner, glanced out the window at the rain, and searched her heart and soul for the hope of some emotion, some attachment, some sense of purpose, something, anything, just one thing.

An hour later Marianna pulled into the parking lot of the bed and breakfast determined to put an end to her defeatist thought process, one way or another.

As she stepped into the lobby, she saw John and Jamie sitting on the couch watching the door. The anxiety on their faces spoke volumes. She stared at them. She told herself she should feel regret, guilt, or, at least, something that she'd caused them so much worry. She tried to force the emotion. She tried to pretend like she felt something, but it was just too exhausting.

John spoke first. "Marianna, I've been so worried about you."

Before she could respond, Jamie said, "I think you need some help, Mare."

Marianna nodded as a tear slid down her cheek. "There's no use. No use to any of it."

John put his arms around her. "We'll figure it out. Come home where we can figure it out together."

Marianna sighed, took a deep breath and counted to ten, before releasing a slow controlled exhale. "I just don't know if I can. It's all just so pointless."

John released her. "Maybe, but we need you in our pointless little lives."

Jamie added. "You're not alone. We're here for you." She smiled. "Remember when you told me that when it all feels pointless, we're on the verge of a breakthrough?"

Marianna smiled. "Sounds like pop psychology to me."

"Yep! That's what I said." She stood back and made a sweeping gesture up and down her body. "But look at me now."

"Well, if you survived the nothingness, I guess I have no excuse for giving up."

John and Jamie both smiled and exclaimed their college rallying cry. "Nothing can beat us!"

Marianna smiled at them both as they linked their arms through hers and responded even though her heart wasn't totally convinced. Knowing John and Jamie understood gave her a reason to keep trying... At least she hoped it would. "Nothing can beat us!"

The Fall

I stepped out of the trees to look over the cliff. I'd been here years ago when I'd felt the despair of yet another failed relationship coupled with a complete dissatisfaction with my career trajectory. I stood on the precipice and looked down thinking how easy it would be to fall. The earth beneath my feet was crumbly and rocks slid down every time I moved my feet. The boulders beneath would kill me before I hit the bottom. I sighed.

I turned my head to look at the tree I'd embraced as I thought about falling. At the time it had looked as if it would tumble down the cliff any minute with its roots sticking out of the ground. Still, its leaves and branches had been healthy. A tear gathered in the corner of my eyes as I noticed it had been struck by lightning and split down the middle. Its top was no longer crowned with green leaves blowing in the wind. It was as bald as I.

I sat on the edge of the cliff and played with an exposed root thinking about all that had happened in the intervening years. I smiled as I remembered the moment I heard a voice ring out through the trees with such determination that even the birds stopped singing.

A moment later a beautiful blonde burst through the trees to stand near me. As I stared at her, my heart leaped. I fell in a way I certainly hadn't expected when I started out that morning.

I stared over the edge and wondered if life would be better for her if I took that fall now... Just as the thought crossed my mind, I heard a voice behind me. "Madge, no, it wouldn't. Don't even think it." I turned. Ursula stood there looking as radiant if now graying as she had that day all those years ago.

"How did you…" I choked back a sob.

"Because I know you, my love." She sat down beside me and took my hand in hers. "We're in this together. There's only one kind of fall for us."

I looked into her eyes and fell in love all over again as we whispered quietly, "Falling into us."

Today, My Love, you finally fell from my arms… I stood in the funeral home as some man who'd never known you talked about how your soul was finally at peace. I glared at him barely able to hold in my contempt, the contempt I knew you would've shared. I should've been stronger when your family insisted on having a minister speak, but I couldn't divulge that one last secret you kept from them. I know you wanted to protect them.

Then I stood up to speak… By the way, they introduced me as your close friend instead of your life partner. I know that would've irked you, too. I looked out at the crowd and regaled them the story of how we met right here on this spot where I now write these words.

As soon as they handed me your urn, I headed here to spread your ashes in this place just as you asked. That hike is much more difficult in a skirt, let me tell you. Standing here beside the tree you hugged so tightly as I burst through the woods, I'm so glad you didn't fall that day. I'm so glad you decided getting to know me was worth falling into my arms. I remember your feet slipping on the loose dirt and rocks as you worked your way back up to find firm footing. I remember you almost tripped over that exposed root as you stared at me. I remember I reached for you then as I do now. All those years ago that tree so full of life and determination to hang on to the side of the mountain, just like you. Now the tree, damaged by a lightning strike, is broken and dying, perhaps already dead. But I will hug it after I spread your ashes under it just as I promised you I would.

And, no my love, my dear, sweet Madge, I won't fall today. I remember what you said to me about facing life without you "Hug the tree until someone reaches out to take your hand." I don't want anyone's hand but yours. When I do finally fall, my ashes will join yours here so we can nourish the new seedling growing between the exposed roots of our falling tree... Where I fell harder than I'd ever fallen in my life right into a life with you, a life so much better than I'd ever imagined possible...

Falling into us was the best thing I ever did. Your Love, Ursula

Without Reason

Balinda sat on the edge of the sofa and stared out the window just as she had every night for the past year and a half –ever since September 11, 2001, the infamous tragedy forever to be etched in everyone's mind as 9/11. Every time her husband left the house, she feared for his safety. She constantly fought her fear he would disappear without a trace and not by choice.

None of her friends understood her fears. Maybe her fears were irrational, but every time she thought about the things she heard on the news – the distortion of facts, the gross generalities, the misconceptions, the irrational excuses for hatred and bigotry, the excusing of inexcusable behavior – her fears only heightened.

Talk shows, pundits, politicians, and other "people in the know" managed to plant the seeds of fear, fertilize them, and grow them at super speeds to super heights with super fruitfulness. Far too many people took this fear and ran with it imagining danger in every person who looked or sounded different, who expressed a different belief or opinion than theirs, or who fit some stereotype.

In the weeks following 9/11, she became hypersensitive to the looks that seemed to linger a little too long when she walked through the mall, down the street, or through the grocery store aisles with her husband. At one time, she would've assumed people were admiring his handsome face and engaging, gorgeous eyes, but now she feared they were making assumptions about his ethnicity and what that ethnicity meant.

The strange looks and the subtle differences in the behavior of people who'd known them for years – some only in a professional capacity but had known them just the same hurt her far more. The sudden forced politeness where before there'd been genuine friendliness – or at least what they'd perceived as genuine.

In one breath good friends, many long time friends, offered support and in the next asked questions with innocent tones and accusation in their eyes. As if she or her husband possessed the power to do anything about the actions of a group of people they'd never met and to whom they had absolutely no connection. She tried to convince herself, in order to keep her friends, her life as she knew it, she imagined those attitudes.

Suddenly, gaps appeared in their social calendar. She wanted to believe their friends were just spending more time with their families. She tried to give them the benefit of the doubt, but when her emails and phone messages went unanswered – unacknowledged even – her excuses for her friends sounded increasingly lame, even to her.

Beneath all her fears, making her even more sensitive, was the ever present one that her husband, the man she loved more than anything, would be the one who got hurt. She could take care of herself. She didn't even care if they made her a target as long as they didn't hurt him. She needed to protect him from the terrible things people could do no matter how much he said she didn't.

It took over a year, but she finally found common ground with some of her friends and let the ones who continued to be hurtful or kept pulling away go. New people trickled into their lives – accepting people open to new ideas, cultures, and beliefs. As much as it hurt to let go of past relationships, life felt better with truly caring people in it. Yet she still wondered who she would call - who she could trust to call - should they face the unfairness of something as devastating to their rights as the PATRIOT ACT.

Her husband probably never thought about these things – at least not as obsessively as she – because he was so secure in who he was. They never discussed it because that would require her to acknowledge aloud just how afraid she felt. She didn't want him to think her paranoid even though she sometimes questioned her own fears as paranoia.

Balinda glanced at her watch, pulled back the green brocade

curtains and looked out again. He was late. He should've been home thirty minutes earlier. She paced the living room and told herself not to panic. He'd probably just gotten engrossed in his work and lost track of time. She picked up the phone and dialed. She listened to the ringing until his voicemail picked up. "Hon, just wondering what time to expect you. Call me. Love you." She deliberately kept her voice casual as she spoke into the receiver. She refused to the let the "what ifs" take over her life.

These mental battles she'd been playing out since 9/11 helped no one. She felt terrified something beyond her control would ruin the life they'd worked so hard to build together. She feared losing the safety of his arms and the security of his love.

When people saw them standing next to each other they'd probably think it ridiculous that she, standing all of five foot two inches, felt the need to protect him with his six foot one inch frame. Yet she did. For weeks immediately following 9/11, she'd barely been able to bear letting him out of her sight. She'd wanted to be right next to him in case her presence would stop someone from doing or saying something hurtful to him.

At first she'd been sure things would get better once passions calmed down and people started thinking rationally again. With politicians keeping people's fears high for political gain, people seemed to find more excuses on a daily basis to excuse behavior that was unkind and uncivil at best and downright cruel at its worst. Rudeness, suspicion, and bad service suddenly were acceptable because the government said people should fear terrorists and that the terrorists they should fear might be hiding in plain sight living normal lives.

She watched a dark car drive slowly past the house for the third time in thirty minutes. She peered more intently at the car and tried to figure out the make and model, but she couldn't in the waning light of early evening. It looked like the same car she'd spotted car parked near their house that morning - the one that sped off as she backed out of the garage. She'd tried to put it out of her mind – to dismiss it as paranoia – but if it was the same car…

She glanced at the clock again. Her heart grew heavier. He hadn't called yet, and he should be home even if he'd left the office just before the phone rang.

Where is he?

The car passed the house again. *What the hell are they doing?*

The timer on the stove sounded. She twitched, shook her head, and tried to shake off her fears. She checked the split pea soup and turned it down to simmer. She picked up a stack of papers she placed on the table earlier and thumbed through them. She needed to keep her mind occupied. Normally, she'd be angry but tonight she felt worried – no, scared, was more accurate.

She read the first paragraph of the report she needed to proof before her presentation the next day without internalizing a single word. She threw the papers down. They missed the table. As they fanned across the floor, she fought back tears.

The doorbell rang. She took a deep breath, held it a long moment, and exhaled slowly. She opened the door and saw two badges, then dark suits, and finally the cold faces of two men who filled the doorway. "Homeland Security, ma'am. May we come in?" The lips of the man to her left moved but the rest of him remained as still as a statue.

"What if I say no?" She shook her long dark hair back and tried to stare into his dark eyes with her blue ones.

The other man offered a cold, patronizing smile, but neither man showed any sign of humanity.

"Is that supposed to mean I don't have a choice?" She stiffened her posture.

"Now you're getting it." The sound came from the first granite face.

"I'm calling my lawyer."

"Go ahead. It'll make no difference."

"What do you want?"

The two men offered only another patronizing smile as a response. They clearly intended to tell her nothing.

The agents walked into the house as she picked her purse up from the table beside the door and started rummaging through it finally pulling out her PDA, so she could look up the number of a lawyer she'd met at a business conference a few weeks earlier. As she clicked the stylus against the screen, she saw one of the agents pick up the papers she'd dropped on the floor only a few minutes earlier. "Hey, those are confidential papers from my job."

He didn't even glance up as he kept reading them. A third man dressed in a dark suit stepped through the open front door, and placed a box on the floor. The first man dropped the papers in the box. He reached over and took the PDA out of her hand and put it in the box. "Hey, I was looking up my lawyer's phone number."

He turned his back on her and signaled for the agent with the box to take it to the kitchen. She watched another agent walk through the door with more boxes and follow the first agent straight to their home office.

She turned first one way; then the other. *Which one should she follow?* She started toward the office. A crash in the kitchen changed her mind. She turned on her heel and walked into the kitchen. She placed her hands on her hips. "What the hell…"

She stopped mid-sentence as she saw the agent examining their food with a spoon and his gloved hand while the agent with the box dropped the knife she'd used to chop vegetables for dinner into the box. "You're ruining our dinner."

Then she turned her gaze to the other agent. "The knife I used to cube the chicken is in the dishwasher. Do you want it, too?" She refused to control the sarcasm in her voice.

When the agent opened the dishwasher, she rolled her eyes.

She walked down the hall to see what the agents in the office were taking. Halfway there, she stopped. The agent had gone straight to the office while the other one had headed straight to the kitchen. They'd known exactly where they were going. She stepped into the office. Anger flashed in her eyes. "Damn you. You've been in my home before, haven't you? What have you done? Tapped our phones? Installed cameras? Just how much of our privacy have you invaded? I thought we still lived in America. This is ridiculous. You have no right…" Her voice broke as tears filled her eyes.

The agent who'd carried in the boxes, and who looked younger than the others looked straight at her. "The PATRIOT ACT." Then he turned his back to her and resumed putting the items from her desk in one of the boxes.

She stared at him. "The PATRIOT ACT." That was all he had to say as if that was enough to explain treating her like a criminal.

A tear broke through and slowly rolled down her cheek as she turned and stomped into the master bedroom. *Damn them!* This was *not* the America she'd loved all her life. She stood in the dark room and looked around. She didn't know what she was looking for until she spotted the reflection of a small red light in the mirror. Surely they hadn't.

She followed the line from the reflection to the wall sconce on the right side, her husband's side, of the bed. She touched the sconce. It was loose. She pulled it off the wall revealing a small recorder – video and audio.

She jerked it out of the wall and stomped toward the office. The first agent grabbed her arm and stopped her in the hallway. She clenched her jaw. "*In our bedroom?* I don't think the PATRIOT ACT allows you to invade our bedroom – our sex life. It can't do that. How dare you." She swallowed hard.

"You're under arrest, Mrs. Abdullah."

"Excuse me."

"You've interfered with a Homeland Security investigation." He pointed at the camera in her hand. "And I'm not required to tell you that much."

She stared at him. "Have you ever heard of the Constitution? You know, the Constitution of the United States? It was created by the founding fathers of America. What about the Bill of Rights? Ever heard of those?"

He took the camera from her hands and directed another agent to put her in handcuffs – they looked like the zip ties her husband used to secure all the cables for their computer equipment and TV components. "This is ridiculous. I want to call my lawyer. That other guy stopped me earlier. Now you're actually putting me under arrest. I want to call my lawyer." She rubbed her wrists against one another and wiggled her fingers.

"That won't be happening."

"Last I checked this was America. Citizens in America have rights. You can't do this." She felt a hand on her back propelling her toward the living room. "I know I have rights. Miranda rights. Call a lawyer. Due process. All that stuff."

The agent leaned close to her ear. Venom dripped from his voice. "Don't count on it. Things are different now, especially for people like you. We'll decide what rights you're entitled to."

"*People like me...* Really? And what people are those? American citizens – born and bred – American citizens?"

The agent turned her around, gripped her shoulders and planted her on the sofa. She watched as they carried out her computer and box after box from her office, a few from the kitchen, and who knew where else. She saw no labels on the boxes.

One of the agents walked back into the house. None of them had bothered to identify themselves, and they were all fairly nondescript. She didn't think she'd be able to distinguish between them in a lineup or even pick one of them out. The agent sat down beside her. "Where's your son been for the past week?"

"At my parents' house." Her voice barely registered a whisper.

"Why?"

"Why? What does it matter?"

The agent stared at her without response. His eyes expressed no compassion or even civility.

She sighed. "Fine. He spends spring break with them every year and another week at the end of the summer since they live so far away. They live in Indiana. You should already know this though since you've obviously had us under surveillance for a while."

The agent remained silent.

"Leave my son out of this. Whatever this is. He's only eight." She looked up at the clock as she blinked back a tear. No way she'd let this idiot see her cry.

Where is Sharif?

He should've been home by now even if he'd left just before her last call and had stopped at the grocery store like she'd asked him to do earlier in the day. She'd forgotten about that. Still, he should be home. She didn't want to let on that she didn't know where he was.

Then again they hadn't asked for him. What if... She couldn't even finish the thought.

She tried not to be obvious when she glanced toward the door to the garage. "Any chance you could uncuff me, so I can get a drink of water?"

The agent went into the kitchen instead of answering. He returned a minute later and held a glass of water to her lips. She took a sip even though what she'd really wanted was to go to the kitchen to get a better view of the door to the garage not that the closed door would've told her anything.

She watched the agents carry out her son's computer and a box with his overlarge toy water gun sticking out of the top. "You're taking my son's toys. What the hell..."

Glancing at the clock a few minutes later, she realized the agents had been searching her home, boxing things up, and carrying them out of her home while she watched helplessly for over an hour. Another tear slid down her cheek. *What is happening to my life? Where is Sharif? Why are they asking about my son?*

The phone rang. She craned her neck to see the caller ID. It was her mother. "Balinda, pick up the phone. You've got to be home." She closed her eyes against the panic in her mother's voice. "Balinda, oh God, I hope you're okay. I'm guessing you can't answer the phone. Two men claiming to be from Homeland Security just took Abdul away."

Balinda straightened her back and struggled to get to the phone.

"I didn't know what to do. They threatened to lock me away, too, for obstruction or some nonsense if I didn't stay out of it. Maybe I should've let them. I don't know. I already called your dad at the firm. He's talking to Bart. You remember him. He's the INS specialist at your father's firm. I know that's not right on target here since Abdul is a natural born citizen, but we didn't know who else to turn to. Please call me. I need to know that you and Sharif are okay. I'm sorry I didn't do more. I love you. Your dad sends his love, too." Her mother's voice choked with tears before the click of her hanging up.

The agent grabbed her upper arm and pulled her to her feet. "Let's go."

Tears streamed down her face. "What are you doing with my son? He's only eight. How could he possibly be a threat? This is ridiculous. Has our whole country gone crazy?" The agent pushed her toward a dark car parked in her driveway. She no longer even attempted to hold back the tears streaming down her face as her voice rose. "He's a child. What could he have possibly done? Why in the hell would our government go after an eight-year-old?"

The agent shoved her into the car. No one spoke to her on the drive to a nondescript building downtown that she thought was abandoned. Once inside, she knew why her husband hadn't made it home. He sat at a desk glaring at yet another man dressed in a dark suit. As they ushered her past him, she heard his confused voice. "He's eight years old. He was born here. In the States. He's a U. S. citizen. He's only been out of the States once when he was four. We took him to visit his grandparents, aunts, uncles, and cousins."

His eyes caught hers as she stared over her shoulder at him.

She felt her butt make contact with a metal folding chair. She could still see Sharif, but she could no longer hear his conversation. The man who'd sat her down walked away without uttering a word. She couldn't stop the flow of tears rolling down her face.

Why are they asking all these questions about Abdul? All this time, she'd been worried about Sharif, and they didn't seem to have the least bit of interest in him besides what he could tell them about their eight-year-old son.

A smiling woman in a navy suit approached. "Mrs. Abdullah, I need to ask you some questions."

"Do I really need to be cuffed?" She turned half-way around in her seat.

The agent removed the cuffs. Balinda rubbed her wrists briefly before wiping the tears off her cheeks. The agent handed her a tissue. She blushed as she blew her nose realizing privacy wasn't an option.

The agent settled into her seat and slid her legs under the desk. She opened a notebook and scanned a few pages covered with notes and questions. Balinda wondered if the agent's actions were supposed to make her nervous. If so, it wasn't working. She felt too angry about the way her family was being treated and too worried about her son to be nervous.

"Okay, Mrs. Abdullah, why did you send your son away?"

"I already told that agent my son always spends spring break with my parents. He doesn't get to see them very often."

"Do you know who your son talks to online?"

"Of course, he and his friends exchange emails and instant messages all the time."

"Is that all?"

"Well, he also talks to his cousins."

"Where are his cousins?"

"Ohio, Illinois, Indiana, Syria, Jordan, and Palestine."

"You mean Israel."

"Whatever." She wasn't getting dragged into that argument.

"Do you monitor his instant messages?"

"Not always, but he knows his communications can be checked at any time." She looked into the lady's eyes. "Why are you so concerned about the conversations of an *eight-year-old boy*?"

"I'll ask the questions."

"But this is silly. Even if he said something stupid, he has no way to do anything. Whatever you think he said they're only words. He's just a kid."

"What sites does he visit on the Internet?"

"We have certain sites locked out completely and others he's only allowed to visit with adult supervision."

"How often do you check up on his Internet traffic?"

"I don't know. Periodically. Whenever we feel it's necessary. Are you saying he's visiting sites he shouldn't?"

The agent gave her a sideways look. Balinda sighed. "I know. You're asking the questions."

Four hours later after listing her son's classes, his friends, his hobbies and interests, and all his family members, she was worn out and frustrated beyond redemption. They'd finally let her have a glass of water two hours into the interrogation. She was starving and knew Sharif had to be as well. He wasn't much of a snacker, so she assumed he hadn't eaten since around noon. She watched the agent review her notes and questions.

"Look, you have enough information to write my son's biography. What else could I possibly tell you? He's a good boy. He makes good grades, has good manners, is respectful to adults, plays nicely with his friends, keeps his room clean and organized. What else can I tell you? Let's see. His teachers love him. He willingly donates his old clothes and toys to charity. He helps around the house."

The agent stared at her like she'd lost her mind.

"Oh, and if you want to know about his finances, he gets ten dollars a week in addition to his lunch money. Of that money, he puts a dollar, at least, in his piggy bank. At the end of the every year, he has me put the money in his savings account for college. Let's see. That's about it, I think. Is that enough? It's going to have to be. There's nothing else."

"Does he spend much time with his father?"

"I don't understand your question. We're all together all the time. We live in the same house."

"Do they do things without you?"

"Some, I guess. They take a karate class twice a week. Sharif coaches Abdul's soccer team. Sometimes I go with them to those, but not always. They like to watch motorcycle and car shows. Sometimes I get bored with those. But that just makes Sharif a good father. We like to support Abdul's interests, so he knows we believe in him." She ran her hand over her hair. "What is it you really want to know? You have to already know the answers to this stuff. You've had us under surveillance."

"How's your son coming home from his grandparents' house?"

"They are driving him home at the end of the week and staying with us for a few days before driving on to visit friends."

"So does he always stay with them this long?"

"Damn, lady, how many ways can you ask the same question? The answer hasn't changed in the past hour. You just keep asking me the same things. Read your notes. It's all in there already."

The agent picked up her notebook and walked across the room. While she talked to a group of agents including two of the men who'd removed items from thier home, Balinda turned in her seat and saw Sharif sitting alone staring down at his hands. She wanted desperately to go to him, to hold him, to tell him how much she loved him. He looked up and their eyes met. She saw the pain in his.

How dare they put him through this? He was the most gentle and loving man she'd ever met. They were a normal, loving family. *Why can't these people see that? Why aren't they out there hunting down real threats instead of harassing my family?*

The female agent walked back over to her. She threw a stack of papers on Balinda's lap. "Explain these."

Balinda picked up the papers and looked through them. "They're our bank statements." She shrugged. "What do you want to know about them?" Then she flipped through a couple more pages and stopped. She knew what they wanted but she refused to give them the pleasure of making it easy for them. If they wanted an answer, they would have to ask.

"I think you know, Mrs. Abdullah."

She continued to stare at the agent instead of answering.

"Fine, tell us about those wire transactions to Arab Bank."

"The money goes to support Sharif's parents. What's to tell? It's the norm in their culture for the sons to take care of the parents, so we do our part. That's the whole story." She dropped the papers on the desk. "Sorry to disappoint but there's just nothing here beyond that. And by the way, if you're going to ask me about this fifty different ways, the answers are all going to come out the same because there's simply nothing else to it."

The agents asked the same questions from fifty different angles for hours. Balinda glanced at Sharif from time to time. This was taking its toll on him as well. She watched his posture slouch and his jaw tighten.

Finally, she sighed, looked over at Sharif, then back at her questioner. "Lady, the truth is the truth. It doesn't change because you ask the question a different way. Believe it or don't. I'm past caring what you believe." She closed her eyes. "I have nothing else to say. I've told you the truth. Now I'm done."

At seven o'clock the next morning, she stepped out of the black sedan in front of her house at the same time Sharif stepped out of another black sedan parked in front of the one that brought her home. She rolled her eyes. What a waste of taxpayer dollars to bring them home in separate cars. She felt lucky to be home at all. She'd read about other families who were held for days, weeks, months even in exactly their same circumstances.

She looked at their beautiful home. *Will we ever feel secure here again?*

She ran into Sharif's waiting arms, and they stood on the driveway holding one another until the cars drove away. Sharif slipped his arm around her waist and turned her toward the house. "Sharif, they bugged our home. I found a camera in our bedroom. I'm sure there are more. I don't think we should go in there."

"We have nothing to hide."

"It's not about that. It's about our right to privacy. It's about not feeling invaded, violated."

"I know, hon, but we can't let them run us out of our home. We've done nothing wrong."

"They have Abdul."

"What?" He stopped and stared at her.

"Mom called while they were searching the house. I was handcuffed, so I couldn't answer it. She left a message that two men came and took Abdul."

"That's silly. He's just a child."

"I kept telling them that."

"They asked me a million questions about him. I didn't understand why, and they wouldn't tell me."

"Me too."

"Okay, we've got to call in and take some time off work. Then we've got to go get our son."

Three weeks later, a black sports utility vehicle pulled up to the curb, let Abdul out and drove away. All he said was that he'd stayed at a camp with a bunch of other children where they were asked a lot of questions every day. There was no apology, no statement, no explanation.

After *the questioning*, as they came to refer to it, every time she checked out a book from the library or bought a new one from the bookstore, she wondered if that would bring them back into her home to harass her family. Every time she logged on to the Internet, she wondered if Homeland Security monitored her actions. Every time her son talked online with family or friends, she feared his words would be twisted by watchful eyes.

Their lives changed forever. One can't endure being questioned for hours and having one's child locked away without reason and not have a change in attitude and life. She never again felt the security that living in the United States had provided her since childhood. Her belief that the United States provided a fair and just place where rights were protected and people were treated with dignity was forever abolished. Her faith in the United States had been vanquished.

The lawyer she contacted told her to consider herself lucky to have her family back intact and to let it go. If Balinda pursued the issue further, she warned there was a strong possibility she would just invite more accusations and suspicions that next time might result in her losing her entire family.

Dare to Love

Darelynn stood in line tapping her foot, waiting for the man behind the counter to call her forward. She'd been waiting over an hour, but she wasn't about to leave no matter how long it took. The man behind the counter looked her way and then looked back at his computer. The last customer he'd helped had left six minutes earlier. She knew because she timed him. All three of the other clerks were busy with people.

The man behind her groaned. "What's his problem?"

The man behind the counter looked right at Darelynn with a smirk on his face. She could answer the man behind her. Her skin was a tad too brown for the man behind the counter, but the man behind her had probably never had to deal with that sort of issue. His pale skin, blond hair, and blue eyes didn't tend to bring out that attitude in men like the one behind the counter. Darelynn tried to convince herself she was being paranoid, but she knew better. She'd dealt with men like the one behind the counter all her life.

She sighed and scanned the room again. It was filled with a menagerie of people with all different skin tones. She wondered how the man behind the counter managed to keep his job. She'd watched him work to avoid serving anyone who wasn't as white as him for the full hour she'd been here. She'd also noticed his obvious preference for helping men as if women shouldn't be there.

The person at the counter next to the man who had been

avoiding her thanked the clerk behind the counter and walked away. The lady behind the counter smiled and said "Next."

Darelynn stepped forward glancing quickly at the nameplate for the man who had avoided helping her. "Daniel" with no last name listed. She turned to the woman behind the counter, glanced down to see her name, Clara, and smiled. Clara smiled back, looking exhausted. "How can I help you?"

Before she could reply, she heard Daniel say "Next."

The man behind her in line stepped forward. "About time."

"You know how it is." Daniel said with a nod in Darelynn's direction.

"Not really. All I know is you're going to make me late getting back to work, and that delay will cost me plenty. You've not had a customer here for a good ten minutes."

Darelynn's couldn't keep from smiling as she answered Clara. "Hi Clara, I'm Darelynn Lopez. I just moved here last week. I need to get my driver's license changed, register to vote, and transfer my car registration." She placed a stack of papers on the counter in front of her.

Clara looked up and smiled. "Looks like you're well prepared."

"I hope I didn't miss anything."

Clara flipped through the paperwork, entered some information on her computer, and turned back to Darelynn. Clara took her photo, gave her a temporary license, and her new tags for the car. Darelynn watched Daniel quickly help the man who'd been behind her in line and then ignore two more nonwhite people as Clara processed her paperwork. As she turned to leave, she asked quietly, "Doesn't his reluctance to help certain people make your job harder?"

Clara sighed, "You have no idea. Everyone knows how he is. He has connections though."

"I see." Darelynn smiled and then said a bit louder than necessary. "Thank you, Clara. I appreciate all your help. You sure made my day brighter."

Darelynn stepped outside, pulled out her smart phone and made a quick call. "You were right. There's definitely a problem here."

She hung up as the man who'd been behind her in line disconnected from a phone call, looked up at her and smiled from his perch leaning against a blue Ford F150. "Sorry you were treated so poorly in there."

She smiled. "You picked up on that."

"Yes, it's not unusual around here." He shrugged. "It's not the most inclusive place to live."

"You're not from around here?"

"Not originally. I moved here about three years ago." He looked around. "I'd better go. I wasn't lying when I said the delay in getting back to work would cost me."

"Oh, yes, sorry." She blushed. "I didn't mean to eavesdrop."

"Yes, you did. You're looking for something in there. But that's okay. I get it. My sister's a reporter."

"I'm not a reporter."

He shrugged. "Ain't none of my business, but if you're looking for wrongdoing, there's plenty of it around here to find."

"Really?"

"Yep."

She smiled. "I'd love to hear more about that."

He threw his head back and laughed. "I'm sure you would. I knew you were up to something."

She extended her hand. "I'm Darelynn Lopez."

He shook her hand. "Pleasure to meet you, Darelynn. I'm Randy Mitchell."

She reached into her purse, pulled out a business card with only her name and phone number on it, and handed it to him. "Look, Randy, I understand you have to get back to work, but I really would love to hear more about the wrongdoing around here. You don't seem to take much guff."

He took her card and glanced at it. "What is it you do, Darelynn?"

She smiled. "I work for a human rights organization. We go into communities to help root out injustice and bring it to the attention of the right people to address it whether it be the media, the proper investigative authorities, or lawyers to bring lawsuits. We work with many other civil rights, human rights, and equal rights organizations to promote civil rights and equality in communities and around the world."

He nodded. "Well, that's admirable work, but it must bring you in contact with some pretty dangerous people."

"Sometimes."

"What makes you think I'd help you?"

"You called Daniel on his behavior without hesitation but also without creating a scene."

He shrugged. "Just told the truth."

She smiled. "The truth is good."

He reached into his truck and pulled out a dirty and battered business card. "Sorry it looks so bad, but it's all I got. I spend my days fixing farm machinery and semis. It's hard to keep things clean."

"No worries." She slid the card into her purse and offered him her hand again. "Sorry to take up so much of your time, Randy."

He waved his hand.

She smiled. "Call me if you want to talk some more."

"You can count on it."

As Darelynn drove back to her office, she processed through the events of the morning. She'd gone to the DMV Office with doubts that the reports of the racism were as obvious as they were. They received many complaints that turned out to just be misunderstandings, but this time the prejudice and the interference with the job were so blatant, it felt unreal.

At the office, she wrote up her report and submitted it along with the photos and video she'd managed to surreptitiously take. Daniel's attitude disturbed her, particularly the nasty smile he'd given Randy when Randy called him out. He had no business being in a government job serving the people if he wasn't willing to do his job.

These cases were always interesting and boring at the same time. Several months worth of gathering information, compiling reports, and then presenting the information to human rights organizations, lawyers, and reporters. Her job consisted of exposing the worst of humanity in an effort to make society better for everybody. She wished her job wasn't necessary.

She pulled Randy's business card from her purse and entered his number in her contact list. She'd left out his name and only briefly described their conversation in her report. She didn't think there was a need to involve him quite yet even though she felt confident he could help her move the investigation forward.

Her phone dinged startling her out of her thoughts. She read the text, surprised Randy made the first move. "Hi Darelynn, it's

Randy from the DMV. Meet me tonight at 8pm at the Bluegrass Java & Vine. I have some more information for you."

She walked in Bluegrass Java & Vine at precisely 8pm and looked around. She spotted Randy sitting toward the back of the coffee and wine bar with a dark-haired man. She approached them. Randy stood when he noticed her. As she walked toward him, she looked around, noting the UK Wildcats memorabilia mixed with horse country décor. She looked at the clientele – some in suits complete with ties, others in jeans and flannel shirts, those in work uniforms, and some students. No one seemed to pay much attention to the variety of people in the bar, each lost in their own worlds.

Randy's friend stood as she came closer. He stood an inch or so taller than Randy, his brown eyes met hers. His skin was a tad darker than hers. She smiled as she reached them. "Randy, nice to see you again."

"And you. This is my husband, Trey. I thought he might be able to add some insight into your... what should we call it? Investigation?"

She smiled at Trey, "A pleasure to meet you, Trey."

Trey smiled and took her hand. "And you as well. Randy says you're looking into that racist prick at the DMV."

"Well, yes, I am. I take it you know him."

"All too well. I went to high school with him. He's always had it out for anyone who wasn't a straight lily white Christian, and he's not particularly kind to women either. As you've seen, he doesn't exactly hide his biases."

"How does he keep getting away with it in a job dealing with the public like he does?"

"No one dares complain. His family is too well connected around here."

A waitress appeared and Darelynn ordered a hummus and vegetable plate and a cup of green tea. Randy and Trey ordered soy lattes and a fruit platter. Darelynn waited until the waitress walked away. "So what's his story? Our information on him is very sketchy. In fact, the complaints our office received didn't even include his name, so the office didn't take the complaints all that seriously at first. When I moved here, we had a meeting and decided I'd go in and do a little reconnaissance just to see if there was anything to it. It only took me a few minutes to know exactly who the complaints referred to."

"I'm not surprised. People around here would be afraid to give you his name. His father is one of the local KKK leaders. The family owns quite a bit of land and a couple of businesses around town."

"The KKK? Are you serious?"

"Yep. The KKK around here likes to pretend they're a social organization, and that the bigotry they're known for is a thing of the past."

She looked incredulous. "Are you kidding? They really try to pretend like the whole white superiority thing the Klan is known for is just some ancient forgotten relic of their little club."

"Well, publicly, though no one buys it. All the members practice various forms of racism on a daily basis, through business dealings as well as in their personal interactions."

Their waitress approached the table, and they all fell silent as she placed their order on the table. After they all mumbled "Thank you" and declined when she asked if there was anything else they needed, she walked away. Darelynn dipped her teabag into the small metal pot filled with hot water and stared at it for a long moment.

"So how does the community feel about this?"

Randy spoke quietly, "The community?" He looked at Trey.

"Yes, the community. Well, most of the community prefers not to get involved. This is a working community where most of the people just keep their heads down and go about their business trying to make ends meet and not upset their livelihoods."

"So no one wants to get involved?"

"Most people would say they don't see a need to stir up trouble."

Darelynn looked out the window and watched a couple of cars drive past on an otherwise empty street. She sipped her tea. "Seems to be an epidemic."

"Excuse me."

"This not wanting to stir up trouble. So many people want all the freedom, all their own rights, all benefits, but they don't want to get involved."

"Yeah, well, those people have never had to fight to have the same rights as someone else." Trey sipped his latte. "It's easy to shrug it off when your rights aren't the ones in question."

She nodded. They fell silent, each thinking about Trey's last statement and wondering if they were guilty of shrugging off rights that didn't affect them. Darelynn's job forced her to face that possibility on a regular basis, but she tried to stay alert to those moments.

"Faggot." The voice came from behind Randy just before a short, stocky man in a navy baseball cap stepped close to their table.

Darelynn spurted. "What the…"

Before she could finish Randy was on his feet, standing a good four inches over the shorter man. "Who are you talking to, man?"

The shorter man looked back over his shoulder and up at Randy's face. The surprise on his face indicated he hadn't seen Randy and confirmed his slur was directed at Trey. Trey stood up and smiled at the man. "Is that supposed to be an insult?"

The man in the navy ball cap took a step back as the bartender said. "Come on, guys, we don't want any trouble. Let's keep it civil."

Randy and Trey stood silently watching the man leave the restaurant. Darelynn watched the man who'd left walk past the window toward a black older pickup with a Confederate flag on the back window and Playboy bunny mud flaps on the tires. She didn't even know they still made those. He got in the passenger side and the truck sped away.

Randy and Trey sat back down as she turned back toward them. "That was weird."

"Not really. He's a Klan member. They do shit like this." Randy popped a couple of grapes in his mouth.

"Like what?"

Trey sighed. "Drive around town and look for people to harass. One of his buddies was having coffee when I came in. He left right before Randy arrived, so, more than likely, they thought I was here alone. I sometimes come here to sketch after work before I head home, especially if Randy has to work late. I was sketching before Randy arrived."

"You're an artist?"

"Well, I'm studying to be an architect, so I'm always sketching ideas for structures I'd like to design someday."

"Can I see some of your sketches?"

He handed her a sketchpad. She flipped through it. Buildings, bridges, coliseums, stadiums intermixed with close up details of columns, banisters, and finials filled the book along with many other structures and pieces of buildings. She turned the page and gasped as she came upon a page with a house that stunned her with its modern lines and clear nod to sustainable living. "Wow! What a beautiful house!"

Randy leaned over and smiled. "Yeah, that's our house."

"You live in this."

"Not yet. But we've bought a piece of land, and we're going to build it ourselves."

"Wow! I hope you'll invite me over because I've got to see this when it's a reality." She clapped her hand over her mouth. "Sorry, guys. That was presumptuous of me. I…"

They both laughed. "No worries. I appreciate the compliment of my work. I'm thrilled it touched you so much."

Randy glanced at his watch. "I hate to cut this short. I know I promised to help you, Darelynn, and I will, but 4:30 comes early."

"So will I." Trey added. "Help you, that is. It would be nice to see something done about the injustice around here. I'm not sure how you change people's ingrained, unmovable beliefs, but I have to admit it sure would be nice to live in a town where people really lived the equality and freedom they seem so proud of until it means sharing it with people they don't identify with."

"My organization goes after specific complaints. We then turn the evidence we gather over to the proper organizations and authorities to handle change. Our role is more one of information gathering not policy change or even changing hearts and minds, but I'll take any information you wish to share with me and pass it on."

"Fair enough." Randy said as Trey took the bill from the waitress and placed a credit card in the little folder.

Darelynn reached into her purse to get out her credit card, but Randy put his hand on her arm. "Our treat. We appreciate the work you're doing."

"I heard what you said to Daniel today about your pay getting docked."

Randy threw back his head and laughed. "I wasn't lying. I do lose money when I'm not on the job, but I can afford to. Most of the people in that room couldn't, and most of them also couldn't speak up. I could."

Darelynn spent the next two days doing internet research and visiting the local library. She researched the town's history. She always felt surprised to discover just how often small towns excuse their hatred, vitriol, and violence with words like honor and tradition. She never understood the pride in a tradition that subjugated other people. She created a timeline of the town's history, wrote a brief showing the court's history of not taking violence against minorities seriously, and what she could find about the town's KKK and other hate group activity.

When she walked around town, she drew attention wherever she went. She took note of people who noticed her and wondered how much of that had to do with her being new in town and how much had to do with her skin pigment.

She looked out her office window as she took a drink of coffee. She remembered her parents moving them from neighborhood to neighborhood as they were treated like outcasts every time they moved into a nice neighborhood. They worked hard to maintain their property but dealing with vandalism took its toll on all of them. Darelynn shook off the past and returned to the papers before her. She read through her paperwork looking for holes and making notes where further research was needed. Too many of these stories sounded eerily familiar. She'd seen them far too often in her job and she'd lived them for her entire life.

Her phone rang jarring her out of her thoughts. She answered to hear a rushed voice on the other end. "Darelynn, it's Randy. Trey's in the hospital."

"Oh, no. What happened?"

"He was beaten up and dumped on our front porch. I came home for lunch and found him. He's unconscious."

"I'll be right there."

"You don't have to…"

"Yes, I do."

"I wasn't…. I don't know why I called other than I think it might be related to what you're working on."

"I'm sure it is, but that isn't why I'm coming." She grabbed her purse as she headed toward the door. "I'm on my way. You just worry about Trey. I'll do whatever I can to help."

Darelynn walked into the hospital with purpose in her step. People moved to the side to let her through. She barely noticed the gray walls or the blue and green furniture. She smelled coffee brewing as she walked through the lobby. A coffee shop was on her right and a gift shop on her left. She walked straight past the information desk, past the elevators, and through the door for the stairs. She climbed the stairs two at a time. Randy had texted her Trey's room number, and she intended to go straight there.

She emerged from the stairs on the third floor and turned to take the hall to the right of the nurses' station. Randy approached her from a waiting room beside the nurses' station. "Darelynn, thank you…"

"How is he?"

"Still unconscious. They're still evaluating his injuries. They haven't told me much yet."

"I called a lawyer I work with. She's a friend, and she knows how to navigate these waters. She's going to meet us here, but she planned to call a doctor friend before she came." She pointed toward the waiting area. "Let's sit."

They sat down and Randy stared out the window. They were quiet for a few minutes. The wind blew through the trees as a light rain began to fall. "If he dies…"

"Randy, let's not think like that."

"Darelynn, I want to kill those assholes."

"Do you know who did it?"

"I have a pretty good idea."

"Darelynn." They both turned at the voice.

Randy saw a pretty blonde woman approaching them with three cups of coffee in a tray. She smiled and compassion seems to ooze from her brown eyes.

She extended the coffee. "Coconut milk latte, anyone?"

Darelynn stood and took a coffee. "Thank you, Penelope. This is Randy. Trey is his husband."

"How is he?"

"Still waiting on news."

"I'm a lawyer. I came to make sure this is being handled properly."

"Okay, but I don't think we need an attorney." Randy looked confused. "We didn't do anything wrong."

I know. My job is to act as an intermediary with the police because it sounds like this is most probably a hate crime. I consult with the prosecuting attorney's office on cases where hate crimes might be involved."

"Okay."

"If I'm right, this case is bigger than this incident. We've been watching hate groups and their violence grow in this area for a while. So far, we haven't been able to shut the groups down because the evidence has been flimsy or the victims have been too intimidated to pursue cases. We're hoping we can change that. If we can build a large enough case, we might be able to shut some of these groups down for good."

"And, you're hoping for what here?"

"That Trey can identify his attackers and will be willing to take the case to court. If we can arrest the right person, we're hoping to bring down the whole organization."

"I appreciate the effort, but you can't legislate away hate. Life doesn't work that way."

"I know. But we can hold the haters accountable when they take action. And with any luck we'll give the community a voice to say they will no longer accept hate, or at least violence in the name of hate, within their borders."

A tall man with dark hair, brown eyes, and olive skin tone approached them and nodded toward each woman. "Penelope. Darelynn."

Penelope greeted him with a big smile. "Asim, you got my message."

"Yes, I did. I was called in even before you called though. Dr. Feinstein thought my expertise might be needed."

"So have you seen Trey?" Randy spoke.

"You must be Randy."

"Yes, Dr..."

"Fawwaz, but please just call me Asim." Asim smiled and extended a hand. Randy took his hand and asked again. "Have you seen Trey?"

"Let's sit down."

They sat down in a cluster of chairs near the windows but away from the crowd. Asim cleared his throat before he spoke. "I'm not going to sugarcoat this. Trey took an extensive beating. He has multiple injuries and needs surgery. He's being prepped now, and I'll be going back in soon."

He turned to Penelope. "I made sure his clothing was bagged, photos taken, and forensic samples taken. All of that should be in order for the police. We did our best to preserve the evidence, but as you know our first concern was treating Trey."

Penelope nodded. "Of course."

Asim turned back to Randy. "He's stable, and that's good going into surgery. His right hand is broken in several places. He has broken ribs, a bruised kidney, and a head injury. Right now we're most concerned about internal bleeding in his abdomen. Once we get that under control, I think we can manage the rest of it. I'll know more once the surgery is completed."

Randy's voice broke. "Please don't let him die."

"We'll do our best, but you need to be prepared. He has a living will that includes a no extraordinary measures and a DNR."

Randy blinked several times, but a tear still escaped. "I know. We both do. It's just... I never thought we would be facing this so soon. It's too soon."

Asim patted his hand. "Randy, it's always too soon. Hang in there. We'll do everything we can."

"His hand... He's an artist. He needs..." He gulped. "Without..."

Asim glanced up as a nurse appeared in the waiting area. "We'll do everything we can. I have to go now to start the surgery."

Randy nodded. "Of course."

After Asim walked away, Darelynn turned to Randy. "I promise you Asim is the best at what he does. Trey is in excellent hands. If anyone can save him, it's Asim."

Randy nodded. "What do we do now?"

Penelope answered her phone and listened for a few minutes. "Yes, Detective Kavanaugh, Darelynn called me to advise on the case. I'm at the hospital now with Randy and Darelynn."

She lowered the phone and turned to Randy. "Detective Kavanaugh needs to know if you feel up to answering a few questions that might help the police piece together what happened to Trey?

"Of course. I want to help anyway I can."

Penelope nodded and turned her attention back to her phone as Darelynn squeezed his hand. After a few minutes, she ended the call and turned back to them. "Azalea's been on the force a long time. She would be chief now if she wasn't so damned determined to keep solving cases. She doesn't care for the politics of running the department. But, if she's on the case, it means the department is taking it seriously."

"What do you mean?" Darelynn asked.

Randy smiled. "She's got quite the reputation around here for not letting cases go cold. She was responsible for figuring out that a case of what appeared to be a mother killing her family wasn't as clear as it first appeared. She doesn't give up, and she doesn't accept easy answers just because they're easy."

"I see."

Penelope nodded. "She's also a social justice warrior. Her parents were killed by white supremacists when she was a child and the killers went free while her father was accused of committing a murder-suicide. That moment has driven her her entire life."

"A cop and a social justice warrior." Darelynn smiled. "We need more of those."

"Yes, we do."

Randy sat with Detective Kavanaugh answering questions about his and Trey's life, their friends, their hangouts, their enemies, and how often they were harassed by hate groups. He finally sighed and looked at her. "Look, we're a gay interracial couple. Harassment comes with the territory."

"That doesn't make it right." Detective Kavanaugh looked him, her brown eyes full of compassion.

"No, it doesn't, but we'd be here forever if I started talking about all the harassment we've encountered."

"I understand, but I have to have a place to start."

"I understand that." He looked anxiously toward the entrance to the waiting room. "It's been a long time since Asim took Trey into surgery."

Darelynn squeezed his hand. "Not as long as it feels like, Randy. Surgery, particularly, when there's so much to address can take a while."

"That doesn't help, Darelynn."

"I know, but it's the truth. We need to be patient."

Detective Kavanaugh stood and stretched. "Let's take a break."

Randy turned to her. "No, I'm okay. What else do you need?"

She gently squeezed his shoulder and smiled. "I need a short break. I'll be back in a few minutes."

She walked down the hall, and Randy sat back for a moment. "Actually, excuse me. I'll be back."

Penelope smiled, "We'll be here. If Asim comes back, I'll text you."

Darelynn watched Randy round the corner at the end of the hall before she turned to Penelope. "Do you think there's any chance they'll catch the people who did this?"

"With Azalea on the case, yes. She won't give up. She's been trying to build a case against a couple of different hate groups in this area for awhile. She's arrested several individuals, and they're in prison now. She doesn't move until she's sure the case is strong."

"Do you think Trey will make it? I couldn't get a read on whether or not Asim was optimistic."

"Asim is always optimistic until all avenues have been tried, but I'm not sure."

Detective Kavanaugh stepped back into the area with her phone to her ear and a paper tray of coffees in her hand. She set the coffee down and said, "Yes." followed shortly by "Okay." Then "I'm on my way."

She pressed the button to end her call and turned to Penelope and Darelynn. "I have to go. We have a break in the case. Tell Randy I'll be in touch shortly."

Penelope and Darelynn nodded. "Of course."

Detective Kavanaugh picked up a coffee and walked quickly back down the hall.

A few minutes later Randy returned, and Darelynn filled him in on what happened.

The three sat in silence and sipped the coffee Detective Kavanaugh brought them before she left. Words seemed pointless.

Randy stood up and walked to the window. He stared at the moon and wished for a shooting star to wish on even as he chastised himself for such a foolish thought.

As the night wore on, they took turns walking around, standing at the window, and trying to start idle conversation.

After a couple of hours, Detective Kavanaugh returned. She came in and asked them all to have a seat. "Here's the news. We arrested four men tonight in connection with Trey's assault and battery. There are probably going to be at least two more arrests. We're still questioning them. Not all of them participated in the beating itself. One man drove and another stood lookout. They were bragging about what they'd done at a local bar. We got a call and arrested them as they left the bar. All four have confessed and are telling us who else was involved. One of the four is also sharing about other hate crimes their little group of ten has been involved with. The ringleader works at the DMV, and he's…"

"Daniel." Darelynn said.

"I can't confirm or deny that."

"You don't have to. My organization has been investigating him and his ties to hate groups."

"I see." Detective Kavanaugh nodded. "You and I will need to talk some more about that later. For now, I just want you to know that we've caught them, and with the way things are going I doubt we'll even go to trial. They seem, particularly the ringleader, proud of their actions."

Randy's jaw twitched. "Let me guess. They're only sorry he's not dead… yet."

Before Detective Kavanaugh could respond, Asim entered the room and Randy stood up. He nodded at Detective Kavanaugh. "Hello, Azalea, glad to see you're on the case." Then he turned to Randy. "Please let's sit down."

Once they were all seated, Asim began. "He's stable. There was quite a bit of bleeding, but we got it under control. He's still out. It'll be awhile before the anesthesia wears off."

"His head injury?"

"So far there doesn't look to be any long term damage. He's got quite a few stitches and quite a bump, but the MRI was clear."

Randy nodded. "His hand?"

Asim sat back and sighed. "That one isn't so easy to answer. The damage is extensive. The orthopedist repaired it, but he'll require both physical therapy and occupational therapy."

"I understand." Randy leaned toward Asim. "When can I see

him?"

"I'll have a nurse come get you when he comes out of the anesthesia. Probably in about an hour."

"Okay."

Three months later, Darelynn smiled as she approached Randy and Trey. They sat on a blanket on an empty lot looking out over a lake. She kissed them both on the cheek and looked around. "Wow, this place is beautiful! I can see why you want to build a house here."

"Thank you. So glad you could come." Trey smiled at her and gestured for her to sit down. She sat down beside them.

Then she noticed his sketch pad was on the blanket. "Are you drawing again?"

"A little bit. It hurts, but I'm getting there."

She picked up the sketchpad and opened it to see a drawing of the view in front of her. "Not exactly architecture."

He laughed. "I have myriad interests when it comes to art."

They all looked up as they heard footsteps. Asim and Penelope arrived together and joined them on the blanket. A few minutes later Azalea arrived. Once they were all seated, Randy spoke first. "We want to thank all of you for all your help in finding the people who did this and for supporting us. We have good news."

Trey lifted his injured hand and wiggled his fingers. "First, the orthopedist says my hand is recovering nicely and I should expect to eventually regain full use of it."

"Second, and this is where you come in. We've decided that instead of building our dream home here, we want to build a center to celebrate diversity and encourage understanding between people."

"Third, we want you all to be involved in the planning and the organization." Randy handed each of them a folder.

"You don't have to answer now. You can review these materials on your own and let us know."

The cover on the folder showed a rainbow shaped like a heart and the words "Dare to Love" in bold red letters.

They settled down to discuss their new venture as they each read the organization name aloud allowing the sound and the love to ring through the air and drift over the river.

"Dare to Love!"

Deserve Better

Kammi turned slightly and looked up. Andy looked down at her with his brilliant blue eyes. She smiled and reached up to touch his cheek. "How long have you been awake?"

"A while." He shifted slightly still balancing his head on his hand.

"How long have you been watching me sleep?"

"A while."

She smiled. "Wanna share your thoughts?" She let her hand trail down his square jaw line and neck until it landed on his chest.

He moved his free hand over top her hand in its journey. She looked up. "Is something wrong?"

He blinked twice and swallowed hard before he answered. "I just don't want you to go…"

She pulled her hand away from his chest and examined her fingernails. "This won't work. You know it won't. I deserve better than what you're offering, and I won't settle."

"Damn it. I don't want you to settle. I want you to stay. What's so wrong about that?"

"You know damn well what's wrong about that." Anger flashed through her brown eyes. "I told you before. I agreed to this one weekend because I'm selfish enough to need to feel your touch again, but I can't be your whore."

He winced. "That's not fair. I never asked you to be my whore."

"What would you call it? I don't want to be your play thing or your mistress or your bootie call or whatever you want to call it. I deserve love and adoration and someone who wants a future with me, someone who cherishes me. I don't play second fiddle to anyone. That's just the way it is."

"You're not being fair."

"*I'm* not being fair. Who the hell are you trying to kid?" She sat up. The cover slipped down exposing one breast. "There was a time not too long ago when I would've fought to keep you in my life, but I have to love myself first."

"What if you're wrong?"

"What are you saying? You think I *don't* deserve better…" She struggled to keep the pain out of her voice and tears in her eyes as she pulled away from him.

He cut her off. "No! No! No! You deserve the very best. What if you're wrong about what I'm offering?"

She pulled the cover back over her breast and leaned back until she was looking into his eyes. "What? What are you saying?"

"I was afraid you wouldn't show if I told you the truth."

"The truth? You've been lying to me?"

"Not really lying. I just left out one intsy teensy thing."

"What's that?"

"I'm single again."

"What?"

"I was afraid if I told you, you wouldn't show, or that if you did, you would feel pressured somehow."

"What the hell?" She shook her head and ran her fingers through her strawberry blonde hair. "I don't understand. You don't think being here knowing you're going back to her was pressure? What's the matter with you?"

He sat up and rubbed the top of his head. His crew cut didn't even shift position under his hand. "You've been so adamant about not talking about her that I was afraid that if I even brought it up, you'd retreat into yourself."

She opened her mouth to speak as she shook her head. He held up a hand as she squeaked, "I don't…"

"Yes, you do, just in a different way now."

"That's not fair."

He smiled. "Now who's worried about fair?"

She sighed. "I don't want this weekend to end on a bad note…"

"I don't want it to end at all."

"What *do* you want?" Kammi felt a tear that slide down her cheek. She held her breath. *How much do I dare reveal?* She had fantasized about this moment for so long even before they found one another again. She looked over at the closed curtains as she struggled to stifle a sob.

She turned away from him, placed one foot on the floor, and sat up, but he gently closed his hand around her bicep. He waited until she looked at him over her shoulder. His voice barely registered above a whisper. "I want it all. Everything you have to offer."

She needed a moment. Suddenly, she couldn't breathe. She pulled her arm out of his grasp and took two hurried steps. She inhaled deeply and exhaled slowly before she spoke. "I'll be right back. I just need…" She tilted her head toward the bathroom.

He nodded. She knew that he knew she really needed to catch her breath and organize her thoughts, but neither of them called her on her excuse for leaving the room.

She stood in the hotel bathroom and stared in the mirror. *What now? How could she trust this moment?* She feared the past few months forever tainted their relationship.

The mirror showed her the woman she was and the girl she used to be all wrapped up in one. She splashed water on her face as a memory invaded her thoughts. She shook her head. Now wasn't the time to think about their first attempt at a relationship. That could lead to no good. Neither of them was who they were then. Life had taken them in opposite directions, and they'd both changed immensely. Still the thing that had always made them work and that had torn them apart lived. She saw it in his eyes and his smile every time he looked at her.

She remembered the first time she saw Andy. His laughter had caught her attention. It sounded so free and genuine. He hadn't reined it in or tried to play too cool to enjoy the joke. He hadn't tried to look tough or aloof. He just laughed. She smiled as she wondered what the joke was. He'd looked her way and smiled back. She remembered trying to play it cool. She hadn't wanted him to think her forward or foolish, so she'd turned to her friend and started talking. She looked at him again and caught him as he looked at her. She continued to steal glances at him. Every time, he met her gaze with that smile in his eyes, the smile that still both excited and calmed her enough to make her smile even on her worst days.

Eventually, somehow, she never quite knew how, they stood next to each other. She said "Hi" and hated how her voice sounded. She wanted to sound bold and confident and aloof. Instead, she thought she sounded shy and unsure of herself and perhaps even desperate. He smiled widely and returned her "hi". Suddenly, easily, comfortably, they became immersed in conversation. They discussed classes, teachers, their residence halls, their mutual friends, and finally their relationships.

Over the next several days they spent every spare moment together. They explored campus together. They spent hours on the phone. She opened up to him about her childhood. They discussed their dreams. They explored possibilities for a future together. She loved him but felt she had nothing to offer him. He seemed to have led the life she wished for on every birthday, on every shooting star, with every penny tossed in a wishing well. She questioned whether or not he romanticized his childhood. Surely, no one really had a family like he described.

She loved her family, but she accepted they would never be who she wanted them to be. She began to pull away from him. She refused to get involved deeper because she realized he needed to be with someone who could give him what he deserved out of life. Yet, she so desperately wanted to be that woman. And, when they were together, she allowed herself to imagine she was. She pretended she wasn't as damaged as she was. Her irreparable damage left her incapable of being vulnerable enough to truly love anyone.

Kammi closed her eyes. All those years ago, she'd made a decision she'd always regretted, a decision that forced her to question her entire life. Now she faced another decision. He just changed everything. He said exactly what she'd dreamed about him saying. In every fantasy, she'd handled it so much better. She'd been open and honest. She'd made herself vulnerable. But looking at him as he told her what she wanted to hear, she'd frozen just like before. She hadn't known what to say all those years ago when he laid his heart on the table with confidence, and she didn't know what to say now when he laid his heart on the bed with fear in his eyes.

She straightened her shoulders, and walked out of the bathroom. She half expected him to be gone. Instead, he stood by the window in his plaid boxers staring out at the rain. She stared at him. She knew exactly how she felt about him. She knew what she had to do. She opened her mouth to speak and choked on a sob. A tear traced a path down her cheek as she crossed the room and placed her hand lightly on his arm. He turned, and she stared up into his eyes. "Andy?"

He looked down at her face, and she heard the words but couldn't believe she spoke them. "Andy, I want so much from you. In a way, the fantasy of what we could be terrifies me. It makes me afraid that we can never live up to that. I don't want to put that pressure on you. I want everything from you, but not until you're really, truly positive you can and will give me the very best you have to offer. I don't do second. I don't play games. I don't do infidelity. I don't put my time and energy into something that has no chance of giving me everything I deserve in life. I'm not demanding perfection, but I do demand I be treated like I deserve. I've played the "I'll be whatever you want" games and the "I'm not good enough for you" games and the "I'm so lucky you love me because I'm not worthy" games. They destroyed me. They destroyed my previous relationship. I won't play them again. I am who I am. I am happy as I am. I'm not saying I'll never compromise or strive to be a better me. I'm only saying I will never sacrifice myself for a relationship again. I deserve better than that."

"I would never ask you to compromise yourself or change who you are. I never did before, did I?" He gently brushed the tear from her cheek. "Why would I start now?"

"Because that's what people do."

"No, because that's what he did, and maybe even others before him, but I never did."

"Not in so many words."

"Not in any words."

She sighed and stared out at the rain. "Can we say not intentionally?"

He started to shake his head. "I…"

"Let me explain, please."

He nodded, took her hand and led her back to the bed. "It's

warmer under the covers. Let's talk there."

She snuggled under the covers and turned to face him. "When we were together then, I saw something in you that made me wish I was a different kind of woman, the kind of woman you deserved to have in your life. I didn't think I could ever be that kind of woman."

"What the hell is that supposed to mean?" Anger flashed across his face. "You were always exactly the woman I wanted. I never..."

"You saw something in me that I couldn't see in myself. Something I didn't think I could be no matter how hard I tried. It's hard to explain. In a way, you made me want to be a better person, but, yet, you also made me feel I could never be the person you saw."

"I still don't understand. All I ever wanted was you for you."

"And, that's just it. I didn't like me for me, so I couldn't understand how anyone else possibly could."

"Oh, Kammi. Why didn't you tell me this then?"

"I'm not sure I understood it then. By the time I did, we were over." She looked down at the covers and picked imaginary lint from the surface. "And, I was sure you hated me."

"So you've said about a hundred times. What's it going to take to convince you I never hated you?"

She looked up into his face. No trace of his usual humor shined through. She searched his expression trying to decipher it. She wasn't used to him being so serious. She didn't like seeing pain in his eyes, and she liked being the source of that pain even less. "Oh, Andy, I do believe you. I believed you from the first time you told me. I just can't understand it. You have every reason in the world to hate me, to despise me, to never speak to me again."

He wiped the tears from her face again. She sniffled and tried to turn away. She'd never mastered the art of crying pretty like they did in the movies. She felt her nose grow stuffy, her eyes swelling, and the drying tears streaking her face. She didn't want him to see her like this. She didn't want him to think her weak. She wanted him to see her strength and confidence. She wanted him to know she was a woman who loved herself enough to be alone rather than be with someone who didn't cherish her, who couldn't meet her needs, who stayed out of obligation. Those infernal tears betrayed her once again.

"I'm not letting you go." He spoke the words so softly she wasn't sure they were real.

"What?"

"I'm not letting you go. Not this time. I let you walk out of my life before without putting up a fight. This time, I intend to show you just what you and I can be. I will prove to you that you and I can build a future together that works for us both. I will prove to you that I am the man you belong with. I will prove to you that I can be the man you deserve. I will prove to you that you are all the woman I'll ever need."

There were those words....

The ones she'd fantasized countless times hearing him say. Those fantasies she loved, cherished, held in a secret place in heart. The stories she told herself to fall asleep after talking to him even briefly. She sighed and pinched her stomach so hard she almost cried out just to make sure she was really awake.

"What are you doing?"

"What?"

"You just winced like you're in pain."

She blushed and blurted out. "I just wanted to make sure I wasn't dreaming again."

He smiled his brilliant smile, the one that lit up his whole face and hugged her tight. "Then maybe I need to pinch myself, but to be perfectly honest if this is a dream I don't want to wake up... ever."

She smiled. "Me either." He kissed her with a kiss that somehow managed to be soft, deep, gentle and passionate all at once. "We sound like something out of a bad romance novel."

He shook his head. "I don't care. I want you to know how I feel."

She reached up, placed a hand on his cheek, and said. "It's going to take a whole lot more than words."

"I know. I know. Words are cheap, and I need to show you I mean what I'm saying. I've tried this whole weekend. Hell, I've been trying for months, but with everything between us, with the situation we found ourselves in, with, well, the damned distance itself, it felt like everything conspired against us. I admit it. I was scared. I was scared how you would react. I was scared you didn't want the same things I want. I was scared if I made that move, you'd laugh at me. So, I opted for what felt like the safer route. Express what didn't make me feel vulnerable. Express what didn't put you in an awkward situation. Express only what I thought would keep you from running away."

"But that almost made me run away. As much as I wanted all we were expressing, I wanted more, and I was afraid you didn't. I hesitated to tell you what I really wanted."

He laughed and hugged her to him. "Have we learned nothing? Were we really doing pretty much the same thing we did all those years ago?"

She sighed. "You were more expressive then. You were willing to risk opening up to me. I just couldn't do the same with you. You intimidated me with your expressiveness. I had no idea how to respond to that kind of openness. I wasn't used to that. People I knew lied, cheated, betrayed, manipulated, but they only pretended to be open. When someone was as open as you were, my experience said they were hiding something. I was afraid of what would happen when that something was revealed. Or worse yet when it wasn't. Then I would have to figure out how to be in that kind of relationship, and I didn't know if I could ever learn to trust… Well, honestly, I knew you deserved my trust, and I felt so guilty because I honestly didn't know how to trust anyone…"

"And now?"

"Oh, I know how to trust now."

"But are you still afraid to trust me?"

She hesitated, looked down, then turned her head to look into his eyes. "I do trust you. Even given how this whole thing started, I trust you."

"But?"

"But what?"

"There's a but in your voice."

She inhaled and exhaled slowly. "I'm still a self-preservationist. I have to admit there's a part of me that thinks if you could do this with me, you could do this to me."

He smiled. "Thank you for saying it. You did this with me, too, so I get it."

"Difference is this is the first time I've ever done anything like this, and I only did it because it's you."

"I know that. And, honestly, I trust you even given the circumstances of our beginning."

"Which beginning? This is our third, or is it the fourth?"

"All of them. Any of them. We've never come together under the best of circumstances."

"Well, I wouldn't say that." She giggled, raised an eyebrow, and smiled.

"That's not what I meant."

"Yeah, but I couldn't resist. The mood needed lightened a bit."

"But, wait a minute. What do mean when you say "difference is"? You think I make a habit of this."

She shrugged and looked away from him. He gently hooked a finger under her chin and turned her to look at him. "Seriously. Tell me. Do you think I make a habit of this?"

"I don't know. I'm not sure I want to know. If you don't, that means this is special for you, too. If you do, I don't want to know I'm just another woman you're playing…"

"Stop right there. I do *not* make a habit of this. And, this is special. You're special. When the hell are you going to understand that? You've always been special to me. That will never change. If you say you never want to see me again and walk out that door right now, I will be devastated, but you will remain special to me."

Kammi reached up and pulled his face toward her. "Kiss me."

He started to speak, but she put her finger to his lips. "Please, just kiss me. I know we need to figure this out, but right now I *need* you to kiss me."

His lips touched hers gently, softly. He pulled back and looked into her eyes. She tilted her head up inviting his kiss. He pulled her close and kissed again. His kiss asking what she really wanted from him. She answered with a full, slow, passionate kiss that joined them to one another. When their lips parted, they both gasped. They smiled at each other. "Does that tell you what I want?"

"Oh, Kammi, tell me this isn't a dream."

"Hhmmmm! Now, I think I would likely say that even if it was a dream since that's what you want to hear." She smiled.

"What do we do now?"

"I don't know, but I knew when I came here this would either give us closure or launch us anew."

"I did, too. It's why I put it off for so long. I was scared it would the former rather than the latter. And, I didn't want that." He sighed. "That was the one thing I was sure I didn't want."

"As much I'd love to just sit here and talk, I'm starving, and I need some fresh air and sunshine. Let's go for a walk and find a restaurant."

"So we're really doing this thing? You aren't going to back out, run away, disappear on me again?"

"I'm here because I want to be. I have no plans to back out, run away, or disappear. I can't promise what will happen in the future. All I can promise is that I really want this to work. I really want something real with you. I know we bring some baggage along with us, some we created together, some we created separately, but I think we have a real chance at being happy together. So, I am here to figure us out. I am here for the long haul. I promise you I will give this my best. And, I am no quitter."

"That I know. Quitting was never your style."

"So what about you?"

"I'm still trying to figure out if I'm awake."

"That doesn't answer the question."

"I have no intention of giving up. I've wanted us for as long as I've known you. I have no intention of screwing that up now."

He kissed her again pulling her close to his body. All thought of food, sunshine, and fresh air disappeared as they melted into their shared passion.

Take a Chance

Temira stared at the ice in her glass of Woodford Reserve
Double Oaked Bourbon as it slowly melted. She looked around the
bar and sighed. The men all appeared the same - desperate, middle
aged men who looked like they didn't know what to do next. She
sighed. *Why did I come back here?*

She stirred the ice with her finger. The cold against her finger
barely registered. She stared into the glass as if it held the secrets
that would move her forward. Life messed up even the best laid
plans. She'd never expected to be alone again. Yet here she was.
She'd given it her best. They both had. Somehow, they'd even
made it work. Quitting had never been their problem. Their
problem... Well, they'd had their share of those, but in the end
they'd always found each other again. That possibility no longer
existed.

She needed to learn how to be alone again. She sighed.

The last time she'd been single, she'd loved it. In fact, her
single days were the last time she remembered feeling genuinely
happy. She'd also been young and the possibilities in front of her
endless. She no longer knew what she wanted. She sipped the
bourbon.

Her life was her own again. She could set her own rules.

"Excuse me." A somewhat familiar voice drawled. She looked
up at the blue eyes of a smiling, freshly-shaven vaguely familiar
face.

"Sorry." She shifted to the side thinking he wanted a better vantage point to catch the bartender's attention.

He laughed. *Damn, that laugh was familiar, too.* She stared at him. Finally, he spoke again. "Actually, I was wondering if you would mind if I sit here."

She looked down the row of barstools and shrugged. "Sit wherever you like, but no that seat's not taken if that's what you're wondering."

"So you're here alone." His tone wasn't quite a question nor a statement.

She blinked back a tear. She hated that word "alone". It sounded so...well, lonely. Odd because she used to love the word back when it represented freedom and independence. "You could say that." She swallowed hard.

"I could say that or it's the truth?"

She cocked her head to the side and smiled. "Damn, I thought you were familiar."

"Excuse me."

She smiled. "So you don't recognize me either?"

"Well, to be perfectly honest, you look like someone I knew in college, but we've not been in touch in years. Last I heard, she got the hell out of this place and vowed never to return."

"Yes, I did."

He stared at her for a long moment. She smiled. "Oh my God, Temira, is that really you?"

She laughed. "Yes it is, Burke. It's really me."

A man approached them and said, "So, Burke, is it her?"

She laughed so loud the man's expression turned quizzical. "So you did recognize me?"

Burke blushed three shades of pink, so she nudged him with her elbow. "It's okay. I would've done the same thing if I'd seen you first."

The stranger laughed. "Hi, I'm Kane."

Temira shook his proffered hand. "I'm Temira. Would you like to join us?"

Kane looked at Burke. "Another time. I think I'll leave you two to get reacquainted. Besides I have to meet someone in a little while."

Temira smiled. "Are you sure you can't join us for one drink?"

"Thanks. I appreciate the offer, but no thank you. You two are going to start talking, and I'll just feel clueless or you'll spend all your time trying to clue me in. That won't be fun for any of us. I'm sure I'll get the opportunity to get to know you soon, Temira." He smiled and turned to leave. "Later, Burke, and don't forget. Ten in the morning."

"Yeah, yeah, yeah, I'll be there."

Temira smiled and took the last swig of her bourbon and signaled the bartender to pour her another. She looked at Burke. "Want one?"

He hesitated. "Well, I was drinking beer."

She crinkled up her nose. "Wuss."

"Fine." He looked at the bartender. "What she's having, please."

She laughed. "Peer pressure. You give in too easily. I don't remember that about you."

"I do not!" He shook his head. "Not about the important things anyway."

"Sure, you don't." She teased.

He stared at her for a long moment with a serious expression. "Temira, what's going on with you?"

"What do you mean?"

"When I first noticed you, you looked so sad, lost almost. Definitely lost in thought. I wondered if something bad had happened. You were looking around this room like you were looking for someone you knew you weren't going to find. You looked like you but not. Now, I can see the girl I remember in your actions, your smile, your eyes."

"Well, aren't you both observant and poetic?" Her voice carried more than a bit of an edge.

"Whoa! I didn't mean to piss you off."

"You didn't." She looked into her glass. "Not really. It's just that I finally forgot for a few minutes…"

"Forgot what?"

She sighed and blinked back tears. He put his finger under her chin and gently turned her head until he gazed in to her eyes. She looked into his and felt an odd sensation in her stomach. *What the hell…* "Forgot what, Temira?"

She swallowed hard before she finally spoke, her voice barely above a whisper. "The reason I'm here."

He waited for a bit. The song playing changed from a pop song to a dance tune. "And that is?"

"Burke, please be patient. I've not yet had to say these words out loud. Strange as that sounds. I've practiced them in my head. I've imagined saying them. Never to you." She took a deep breath and closed her eyes. She counted to ten in her head as she exhaled. Then she blurted. "I'm widowed." She opened her eyes. "There I said it. It's said."

Burke stared at her for a long time without speaking. He reached out to touch her shoulder in a comforting gesture. Her mind shouted "No, no, no. I don't want your sympathy. Please don't do that." She said nothing.

"I'm so sorry."

"Why?"

"Excuse me?"

"Why would you be sorry? You never knew him.

"Well, you obviously loved him."

"Yes, but by all rights, you have no reason to be sorry. Actually, you have every reason to hate him."

"Excuse me?"

"Well, I did leave you for him."

"What are you talking about?"

"When I broke up with you, it was because I'd met him. He offered me what you couldn't."

"What was that?"

She paused. She could be cruel. She could be coy. She could be honest. She could flat out lie. "Now probably isn't the time to have this conversation. I'm lashing out at everyone right now."

"I thought we broke up because… Actually, I can't remember why we broke up. What I do remember is that you had plans, and I didn't seem to be a part of those. No man did."

The song playing in the bar changed again. As Abba sang the first few lines of "Take a Chance on me", Temira looked away and Burke looked down at his glass. Neither of them spoke, but Temira was sure he was remembering the same night she was, the night they listened to it while they made love in her residence hall room. Neither of them knew then it would be the last night they spent together.

She sighed. "Yeah, that's true to a large extent. I was moving on with my life, and I didn't think I could wait for you to grow up." She clenched her jaw. "See, now that's what I didn't want to say. We were just at such different places. I was starting a career. You were still in school. You were more interested in partying with your friends than in preparing for the future. And, I didn't have the time or patience for that stuff anymore. I was just ready to move to the next place in life, and you weren't."

"And he was?"

"Yes, when I looked at him I saw a man. When I looked at you, I imagined the man you would become." She examined the ice in her glass. "I'm sorry."

"Don't be. You were right. We were at different places. Reconciling that would've been difficult. Did he make you happy?"

She looked into his eyes. "That's a loaded question, Burke. We were happy together for the most part. But, one thing I've learned is that no one person can make another person happy. That's too much responsibility to put on anyone, and it will destroy a relationship. Happiness comes from within. Anything else is only a facsimile."

He smiled and chuckled softly. "How very philosophical of you. Is that what you're telling yourself right now as you grieve?"

"Wow, you don't wear sarcasm well, do you?"

"Sorry, that came out sounding mean. I really didn't mean it that way." He shifted on the barstool. "Well, I have to admit, this isn't going at all the way it does in my fanta…"

She laughed. "So you've fantasized about this?"

He blushed and stared at the ice in his glass.

"Don't be embarrassed, Burke. I have, too. And, it's not going the way I imagined either."

"Really?"

"Yeah, really." She cocked her head to one side. "In my fantasy, we'd be pressed up against the wall in the alley by now unable to keep our hands off each other. Well, at least you wouldn't be able to keep your hands or…" She focused her gaze on his lips. "well, let's just stick with hands… off me."

"Oh, is that so?"

"Hey, give me a break. It's my fantasy, and being irresistible is a part of that." She shrugged. "What can I say?"

He stared at her. His voice husky when he finally spoke. "You are. That's no fantasy."

"Uh, uh." She shook finger and her head simultaneously chastising and denying. "I don't know what to say. Thank you. But I think we'd better change the subject now. I'm still grieving, remember?"

"Sorry."

"Don't be. I started it."

"Not really. I…"

"Drop it, please." She smiled. "So what about you? Married with a whole house full of children I bet?"

"No. Divorced with a string of failed relationships. Guess I turned into the…what was it you planned to be… a serial monogamist? Right?"

"Yep, that was the plan. Relationships were always a pain in the ass, but I hated dating even more. Damn, I was naïve."

"Not really. It works for some people."

"And for you?"

"Well, I guess it worked better than marriage." He laughed.

"What happened with your marriage?"

"Oh, I don't know. We had a couple of kids. Life did what life does. Monogamy became monotonous. I was more interested in my career than the marriage. She wanted me to be a better husband, a better dad, just plain better. I wanted her to let me have some fun. We started fighting all the time. Then boom, one day she filed for divorce, and told me she was tired of begging me to engage in our life and be a part of the family."

"So you became a weekend dad?"

"At first. Then my job transferred me to another state, and I became kind of a glorified uncle. I was there for occasional weekends and most holidays. I took them to do the fun stuff. It worked for a while. They thought I was the "fun" one. Now, I rarely see them. As my daughter put it, why should she make time for me when I put everything else ahead of her her whole life? My son asked me the other night where I was when he was being bullied in school or when his sister got her heart broken for the first time? Then he quietly told me he's too busy to see me while I'm in town."

"We all live with the decisions we make in life."

He looked at her for a long moment. "You know, most women usually try to tell me that I did the best I could, but I should've known you wouldn't. It's not your style."

She looked away. "Did you?"

"Did I what?"

"Do the best you could've?" She turned back to search his expression.

He was quiet for a minute. "No, I guess I didn't. It seemed to make sense at the time."

"Most things do."

"What about you?"

"What about me?"

"Children?"

"No. After I had a couple of miscarriages, we stopped trying."

"Oh, I'm sorry."

"It's okay. I never really felt that maternal urge most women feel. I figured given my history, mothering wouldn't be my strong point. So I focused on my career." She looked at him and smiled. "Maybe we should've kept the conversation on those fantasies... This is getting a bit depressing."

He laughed. "You're right. It is. What do you do?"

"I'm a psychologist, so I listen to people's problems all day. It's a blast. Let me tell you." She smiled and tipped her glass toward him. "You?"

"I'm a manager with a company that builds top secret equipment for the military. We also have some civilian clients, but our main work is for the Department of Defense."

"I see. That's impressive."

"It's really pretty boring. I used to be implemental in research and design, but my promotion means I mostly just push paper around and give talks at seminars these days." He shrugged. "It's a paycheck. At least you get to hear interesting stories."

"Not really. You'd be surprised how similar the stories often sound. People have a lot of the same issues stemming from the same kind of history. It's really quite depressing not to mention monotonous."

"But at least you're helping people."

"I guess. Sometimes it's hard to feel that way. And, I could say that at least you're helping to protect our nation."

"If you say so. I mostly just think of it in terms of getting the next contract signed and the obligations therein met."

"Ah, adulthood. Isn't it grand?"

He signaled the bartender to pour them both another drink. "Remember when we used to sit in your dorm room and talk about the future? I don't think either of us imagined this conversation."

"No, we didn't. I think most of our thoughts then were about the freedom to do the things we thought we weren't allowed to do."

"Like have sex whenever, wherever we wanted."

"Well, I do believe we found ways around that one all the time." She glanced up at him for a second and then examined the ice in her glass again as if it could predict her future. A couple more and that prediction wouldn't be difficult to make.

"Yes, we most certainly did." His voice grew husky with the memory.

She leaned back slightly and downed the last of her bourbon. "Take me for a walk?"

"Seriously?"

"Yeah, seriously."

"Just like old times."

She shrugged. "I guess."

"Sure." He downed his drink and signaled for the check.

She started to protest but changed her mind when she saw the set expression on his face.

They left the bar walking side by side. She loved summer evenings but couldn't remember the last time she'd actually gone outside to enjoy one. She looked up at the stars twinkling and wished they were somewhere out in the country where the stars would be more visible. They walked the familiar streets noting the similarities and the changes since life had taken them in different directions.

Walking in the city with Burke felt very different than walking around campus had all those years ago. For one thing, there were a lot more people milling about. For another, she wasn't exactly dressed for a walk in the black and white geometric print dress and black open-toed pumps she'd worn for the memorial service. She really should've changed before she popped into the bar, but she hadn't felt ready to return to her room alone.

"Hey, Temira, where'd you go?"

"Uh? What? I'm right here."

"Sure you are. I can still tell when you're thoughts are in the stars."

She laughed. "Actually, they kind of were. I wish we could see the stars like we used to when we walked on campus, but I was also thinking that maybe I should've changed after the memorial service. I'm not really dressed for a walk." She lifted one foot turning the three-inch heel of her shoe toward him.

"The service was today? Geez, when you said you were widowed, it didn't dawn on me that it was that recent."

"Yeah, it's only been a week. You don't think about things like how to handle funerals and such when you live a long distance from family. He wanted to be cremated, so I took care of that. Then I brought his ashes here. You always think people will come to you in a situation like this, but it really doesn't work that way, especially when all your family is a couple thousand miles away. And, when I get home I've got to go through this again for our friends and co-workers there. Unbelievable to have to have two memorial services for someone. I just can't fathom it. Yet, everyone expects it. It's crazy."

"Wait. You've got to do this again? Isn't that going overboard?"

"Well, it seems like it to me, but our friends are insisting on a chance to remember him, to say goodbye. At least I've got help with the arrangements on that one. A couple we'd been friends with for years is hosting the memorial – more of a party really to honor him."

"I see."

"Do you?"

"Well, sort of." He paused. "You seem to be handling the loss well."

She shrugged. "I was sitting in a bar determined to drink enough to pass out when I got up to my room, so I wouldn't have to think about sleeping alone. I'm not so sure that's handling it well."

"I guess not."

"No guessing about it. I don't drink often anymore, so it wouldn't have taken much more."

"Are you drunk?"

"No, but I should probably eat something. All I had today was a few bites between accepting condolences."

"There's a great little restaurant around the corner."

"Have you eaten?"

"No, I was supposed to have dinner with Kane and his friend, but then I saw you at the bar."

"Oops! Sorry. It didn't even occur to me you had plans."

"Don't worry about. I'd rather catch up with you. Really, I would." He flashed a conspiratorial grin. "Trust me."

"Okay. Nothing too fancy. Nothing too loud. Just something casual with great desserts."

"I know just the place, but it's a bit more of a walk than the first restaurant I mentioned."

"That's fine. Let's go."

"So tell me about your husband?"

"What's to tell?"

"I don't know. You were married a long time. There had to be something that kept you there."

"Burke, I don't know." She looked up at the sky. "The moon is beautiful tonight."

He looked up. "Yes, it is."

"Look, I know you're trying to do the right thing. Give me a place to talk through my grief, but I really don't want to. I spent the entire day focused on him, his life, and his death. I just need a break from it. Do you understand?"

"Sort of." He paused. "Okay, fine. Just tell me how he died and I'll leave it alone for now."

"He had an aneurism that burst while he was fucking the boyfriend I didn't know about." She glanced over to see Burke's reaction. He stopped and stared at her. "Now, aren't you glad you just had to know?"

"I'm so sorry, Temira. That's must have hurt like hell."

"Yeah, I guess so. I just don't want to think about it."

"I can understand that. I won't ask another question about it, but if you need to talk, cry, scream, rant, rave, vent, whatever, you just let me know."

She laughed. "Thanks. I'll get over it. It's not like it's the first time a man cheated on me."

"Hey, I never did."

"I didn't say that you did." Temira squeezed his hand. "But thank you for saying that. I know I never trusted you like you deserved."

"Maybe you were right to not trust me. Maybe we just weren't together long enough for me to betray you. Besides I did keep secrets from you."

"Oh, really? What kind of secrets?" She nudged him with her shoulder.

"The kind that seem silly now. I wasn't nearly as sexually experienced as I wanted you to believe. You were only the second girl I ever had intercourse with."

"That wasn't nearly as big a secret as you thought. I figured out that you weren't all that experienced the first time. Still, you should've told me. I wouldn't have held it against you." She smiled. "What else?"

"I didn't have nearly as many female friends as you had male friends. I just wanted you to think I was popular."

She laughed. "Well, I didn't have nearly as many male friends as I lead you to believe either, so I guess we both wanted to appear more popular than we were. Well, that's not entirely true. I never mentioned anyone I hadn't actually been friends with. It's just that when you came along, I stopped spending time with most of them. Only a few really close friends stayed. Anything else?"

He looked at her. "I liked you more than you liked me."

She shook her head so hard her hair completely covered her face. "Not possible. I loved you."

"What? I loved you, too. Why didn't you tell me?"

"You never told me." She shrugged. "Besides, like I said earlier I didn't think we could make it work. Our life goals were just too different."

"Sometimes love just isn't enough."

"Yeah, and sometimes it's everything."

Neither spoke for several minutes as they continued walking.

"The restaurant is right around that corner. It's really good. It's a local place, not a chain." He stopped and looked at her. "You might be a tad overdressed."

She cocked her head to the side. "I usually am."

They stepped into the small restaurant. It was clean and cozy.

The furniture was an eclectic mix that looked like it had been bought over many years and perhaps some had even been inherited. Several china hutches contained dishes and knick-knacks. She spotted a couple of metal tables that had a 1960s vibe interspersed in myriad wooden ones. Chairs included wooden, wooden with cushions, and metal with stuffed vinyl seats. Every color in the crayon box – the big box - appeared to be represented, but it all worked somehow. She liked the homey vibe. She searched the room for an empty table and finally saw three, maybe four.

A short, thin, woman with salt-and-pepper hair approached them. Her blue eyes sparkled as she greeted them. She quickly assessed Temira. "My dear, you look like you could use a little comfort food about right now. Lost someone near and dear to your heart, didn't you?"

Temira's jaw dropped for half a second before she regained composure. "Thank you, ma'am. Yes, I did, but how did you know? I didn't think my clothes screamed funeral."

The woman smiled, showing slightly crooked teeth, and patted Temira's arm with her wrinkled hand. "It's not your clothes, hon, though they do seem appropriate for a funeral. It's your eyes. I know that look. I woke to the same one every morning for a year after I lost my husband ten years ago. You'll get through it. Just don't be afraid to let those who love you help."

Temira smiled and nodded but couldn't speak as tears welled in her eyes and her throat felt as if someone cut off her access to oxygen.

"You two just take any open table. We're not too busy tonight, so don't feel you have to rush."

Burke and Temira chose a table near the window. Temira looked around "What does she mean not too busy? This place is packed."

"Oh, this is nothing. I've been here when there's a line halfway down the block. But, that's the way they are here. They never rush anyone. Miss Mabel treats everyone like family."

"You know her by name."

"Oh, yes. You will, too, before we leave. I used to come here all the time when I lived here. Miss Mabel and her late husband, Bill, opened this place a long time ago. It's been here ever since. It's not fancy, but the food is outstanding, and Miss Mabel makes desserts like you won't believe."

Temira smiled as she read the menu. A waitress in her late teens or early twenties approached their table. Her blonde ponytail bounced as she walked. She placed a basket of steaming bread on the table and a plate with half a stick of butter on it. Her green eyes seemed to peer right through Temira as she smiled. "Fresh from the oven. Miss Mabel's famous bread. Taste it. You'll be hooked. I know I eat way too much of it."

Temira had a hard time believing that based on the girl's thin frame. "Thank you."

"I'm guessing you'll need a few minutes to decide."

Burke looked at Temira. "Trust me?"

"To order food?"

He nodded.

"Sure. Why not?"

"We'll have the nightly special."

"Ah, you've been here before."

"Yes, ma'am. Sure have."

"Well, tonight that special is roasted garlic chicken, green beans, mashed potatoes, macaroni and tomatoes, and your choice of chocolate cake or pecan pie for dessert. And, what would you like to drink?"

Temira spoke up. "I'd like iced tea to drink. On the desserts, could we have one of each?"

"You bet." She took the menus and looked at Burke.

"Same."

"Two iced teas, two nightly specials including one each of the specialty desserts coming right up. Enjoy your bread."

As the waitress entered the kitchen, Temira said. "Darn."

"What's wrong?"

"I forgot to ask her if the tea is sweetened."

"It is. Is that a problem?"

"No, I was hoping so, but so often it comes unsweetened."

"Only if requested here. Miss Mabel is a Southern woman through and through."

Temira smiled, picked up a piece of bread, and spread a thick layer of butter over it. She really did miss the South sometimes though she rarely admitted it, even to herself. She bit into the bread. The fresh yeasty flavor mixed with the butter and the bread's crust was just crunchy enough with a center of perfect softness. She rolled her eyes. "My God, that is good."

Burke laughed. "You thought the waitress exaggerated, didn't you?"

"A little bit."

"Never." He bit into his own thickly buttered slice of bread. "We really should come here for breakfast. Miss Mabel makes pancakes and French toast that are absolutely heavenly. Seriously."

The waitress reappeared with their iced tea and another basket of bread. "Miss Mabel just took a fresh loaf of a new bread recipe out of the oven. She wanted you to try it. Let her know what you think. It's a little denser because it's made with whole wheat flour and almond flour. It also has a bit of parmesan cheese and rosemary mixed in."

"Thank you. We will." Temira smiled. "What's your name?"

"Oh, I'm sorry. I usually tell our guests that right up front. I'm Celia. You just let me know if you need anything else."

"Will do." Burke said.

After she was out of earshot, Temira turned to Burke. "Why do I suddenly feel like no time at all has passed?"

"I don't know. I feel like I should be asking you a million questions, but every time I start to I don't know what it is I want to ask."

"I feel the same way." She looked out the window for a minute before she continued. "Maybe tonight we should just enjoy the moment. We have plenty of time to talk about all the ups and downs life has dished out over our years apart."

"I was just thinking something along those lines. Maybe it would be best if we allow things to reveal themselves naturally instead of forcing everything into one conversation like it'll be the last one we'll ever have."

"Absolutely." She finished off her bread and picked up a piece of the new bread Celia had brought them. She slathered it with butter as well and took a bite. "Oh, my God, I've never, ever had a whole-wheat bread that tastes that good. This woman is a kitchen goddess."

Burke took a bite of his and nodded. "So am I understanding this correctly? Did we just agree that we're going to take this beyond tonight?"

"Well, we're back in contact. There's no reason we can't stay that way. Maybe see where things go. I'm not making any promises, but I don't want this to be the last time we ever see each other."

"Then I think we can agree on that."

Over dinner, conversation turned to mundane things. They talked with the kind of ease of people who have always known one another. They talked about their travels. Between the two of them they'd visited most of the world. They talked about old friends they'd kept in contact with and those they wish they'd kept in contact with. They laughed about silly moments in college like the time she got so mad at him she walked the entire campus perimeter in heels to avoid being in her room if he called and how he'd been waiting in her lobby when she returned. Neither could remember what had made her so mad. They avoided any topic that might remind them why she was in town.

When they stepped out of the restaurant, Temira looked down at her stomach. She felt it straining against her dress but it wasn't visible. "After that meal, I really need a walk – the aerobic kind."

"But was it worth it?"

"Absolutely." She turned away from her hotel. "Seriously though I would like to walk for a bit if you don't mind."

"I'd love to."

"But I know you have to work tomorrow."

"My first seminar is at ten, so I'm good. I can sleep in."

"Your conference doesn't start until ten?"

"The conference stuff starts at eight, but there's nothing I need to attend until ten. I promise you, I'm good."

"Okay, as long as I'm not keeping you from your work."

"I've given this talk several times, so I don't need to do any prep work."

They walked in silence for a few minutes. Temira tried to note the changes in town since her college days, but her memory felt faulty.

"So are you going to move back here now?" Burke asked.

Temira turned to look at his profile which didn't betray what he wanted her answer to be. "No, I'm not."

"So you're going to stay where you live now?"

"In Seattle?" She vigorously shook her head. "Hell no. I'm out of there as soon as I can sell the house and all the crap I don't want."

"Oh, where will you go?"

She shrugged. "I'm not sure. Chicago, New York, Atlanta maybe."

"Oh, so back this way anyway."

"Yes. I hate the weather in the Northwest. Most of my friends and family live somewhere in the eastern part of the US. It just makes sense."

"Don't you have friends where you live now?"

"Some but it's not the same thing. They're neighbors, colleagues, friends of convenience. You know?"

"Yeah, it's a different kind of bond."

"Exactly. There's not a single friend in Seattle I could've asked to do this tonight. They would've all had other plans or not gotten the significance of my need. Don't get me wrong. They're all perfectly nice people, but it's not the same."

"I understand. Do you think it will really be different though? I mean maybe the world has just changed and it has less to do with where you live and more to do with that."

"Perhaps, but friends who've been around or have come back around seem to get it more. There's less need to explain every little thing."

"So you don't want to be anonymous?"

"Ah, now there's a question." She smiled. "I could move somewhere where no one knows me or has ever known me and start over completely. Then I could create a whole new history – fiction but new nonetheless – and no one would ever be the wiser. But there's no appeal to me of living a life built on a lie. I've done that. Now I really just want honesty. Raw honesty."

"Raw honesty. That sounds painful."

"Maybe but at least it would be living the truth."

He stared at the street as a few cars passed them. "So, in the name of honesty, what do you want from me?"

"I don't know. I really don't. Seeing you tonight made my heart race. Thinking of the possibilities makes me smile. But we don't really know one another anymore."

"True. I can't argue with that though I do feel like no time has passed. I guess the question is do you want to remedy that?"

"I feel the same way. And, I thought we already answered that question in the restaurant."

"I know. I guess I'm just feeling a little unsure."

"Why?"

"I'm not sure. I keep thinking about how they say you can't go back."

"So we won't go back." She shrugged. "I don't know what we'll be or where this will go, but I know I want you in my life."

"How can we become reacquainted if we don't go back? I mean there were gaping holes we left behind."

She sighed. "I know. And, some of those will be hard to close, but we'll just have to do the best we can. Not going back doesn't mean we never discuss the past. It's our history. It's our starting point. But how we move forward is up to us."

"Our starting point." He nodded. "I think I like that. It sounds more like moving forward than starting over does."

"There's no reason to pretend our past didn't happen. It's not possible anyway. Those things will come to the forefront no matter what we do. We either control how it comes up or allow it to control us."

"I don't want to force it."

"I don't either. What I mean is that when things from the past arise naturally in the course of things, we can choose how we want to deal with it. We can choose to be adversarial or reconciliatory about things. That's under our control."

They reached a small park. She pointed toward it. He nodded. They walked through the park in comfortable silence. After a few minutes, Temira turned and walked toward a swing set. She sat in one of the swings and gently swayed back and forth. "There are some things we never outgrow. The feeling of swinging in a swing is one of them."

Burke smiled and settled into the swing next to her. "I don't know about that."

"You never liked swinging that much to begin with as I recall."

"True enough. I guess I probably liked swings when I was a little kid. What little kid doesn't? But I don't remember it."

She laughed.

"I love your laugh. It was always so hard to coax a laugh from you that doing so felt like a major accomplishment."

"Sorry about that."

"Don't be."

"I have learned to laugh and that laughter is not only okay but good. I know it probably doesn't seem like it."

"Well, given the circumstances..." He stopped and looked at her face.

"Yeah." Temira broke eye contact and looked down at the ground. "Damn, I don't know what I'm supposed to feel right now."

They sat in silence gently swinging. Burke reached over and took Temira's hand. Temira liked the feel of his hand in hers. Tears slid down her cheek. She let them fall. It felt good to let down her guard. It felt good to not need to be strong. Burke squeezed her hand but said nothing. He didn't try to stop her tears. He didn't say anything comforting. He didn't wipe the tears from her cheeks. He simply held her hand and let her feel what she needed to feel.

After she'd cried until she couldn't cry any more, she looked up at Burke. "Thank you. I don't know what came over me."

"What came over you is that you're grieving."

"I guess."

"Temira, it's okay to grieve."

"But I don't feel sad."

"Grieving doesn't have to mean you're sad exactly. Grieving is the process of letting go of what you once had. It's okay to grieve however that grief makes you feel."

"I'm strong enough to handle this."

"I have no doubt you're strong enough to handle this. You've always been strong, sometimes I've even thought you were too strong."

"Too strong?"

"That may not have come out quite right." He paused. "It's just that you were always so afraid of appearing weak that you kept yourself closed off, you isolated yourself even when opening yourself up would've brought you closer to other people."

"Oh."

"Damn, I think I screwed that up again. I'm not trying to insult you. I just always wanted something more with you, and I never could quite breach that fortress you'd build around your heart."

"You didn't screw it up. You're right. I just never realized you saw that." She stared down at her feet and laughed.

"What's so funny?"

She put a hand up to signal for him to wait as she finished her convulsive laughing streak. When she was done, she wiped her eyes. "I'm a widow swinging on a child's swing wearing an overpriced dress and stiletto pumps and crying over a man who saw our relationship as little more than a business contract. And, seeking comfort from the clichéd one who got away... I feel like the biggest cliché of all time. As I looked down, I could almost hear him chiding me for... well, just being me. He never would've understood my need, my desire, to swing. I stopped swinging a long time ago."

"I see." He thought for a moment. "I think that last part was a metaphor."

"Ah... It was both literal and a metaphor. I did quit swinging, but I also quit doing all the things he deemed silly. After all, it was time to act like an adult."

She watched anger flash across Burke's face. It disappeared so fast, she thought she imagined it until he spoke. "Sounds like you gave up having fun."

She shrugged. "More like traded in a free spirited kind of fun for a more sophisticated fun. Isn't that what adults do?"

He shook his head. "Doesn't sound like you enjoyed this so called sophisticated fun very much."

She laughed. "It's not that... It's just different... I miss this kind of simple fun that only relies on doing what I want to do without worrying it won't measure up to some expectation I didn't know I was supposed to meet."

"Isn't that what fun is all about?"

"I guess it's all in how you look at it. Don't get me wrong. I thoroughly enjoyed the fancy dinner parties, the nights at the symphony, the intellectual conversations over overpriced restaurant meals, and always the ridiculously priced name brand clothing that must be worn. Trust me, I like nice clothes, but the novelty of always needing to dress the part takes its toll after awhile. I'm sure you know a little something about it."

He glanced down at his dress pants and shirt. "Well, clothes have never been my thing…"

She smiled and bumped her shoulder against his. "That's not what I meant. I'm guessing you've had to participate in your share of work-related social events."

"Of course, who doesn't?" Burke smiled.

"I know this probably sounds weird. It's not like I'm longing for childhood or anything like that. I just want to enjoy the simple things in life. A walk on a warm summer's night like this, stopping to swing in the swings and not caring if I look ridiculous to other people, sitting in a front porch swing sipping some iced tea, enjoying a cup of hot chocolate in front of a roaring fire, reading a book just for the hell of it, or making love on a rainy afternoon."

He smiled. "Just to name a few things."

"Yeah, just a few."

"Sounds like a nice few."

She smiled and stifled a yawn.

"Looks like your day is catching up with you."

"Yeah, I guess. When it started out, I couldn't wait for it to be over. Now, I can't seem to let it end."

"Temira, as much as I love spending time with you, I think I need to let you get some sleep."

"Sleep… Oh, yes… Time to head back to my hotel room." She paused. "I'm tempted to try to seduce you, but I remember you as too honorable to allow that to happen under these circumstances. And, I do think I might not take honorability well tonight."

"Oh, Temira, we'll have plenty of time for that. When we make love again, it will be for the right reasons and we will both be in the right frame of mind. I don't think we're there yet."

"That's about the sweetest, most honorable rejection I've ever heard."

"It's not a rejection, Temira. I would love to make love to you, and, to be perfectly honest, there have been times tonight when I've struggled to act like a gentleman. But, I care far too much about you to make a move tonight and destroy any chance of us having a future together."

She leaned over and kissed him gently on the lips. "Thank you."

As they left the park, Temira took Burke's hand in hers. She squeezed his hand, and he squeezed hers back. She felt transported back to the time when life offered possibility instead of regret.

Opportunity she'd turned away without a second thought. She smiled. Her grieving wasn't over, but neither was her life.

Burke walked her to her hotel room, kissed her gently on the forehead, then the cheek, and then the lips. "Can I take you to dinner tomorrow night?"

She nodded. "I wish I could, but I fly back to Seattle tomorrow." She paused for a moment. "This isn't over. I promise you that."

He smiled. "You're right about that. I have no intention of ever losing you again now that I've found you."

"You always did know just the right thing to say."

"I'm not trying to charm you, Temira. I want us to make this work."

"I know that, Burke, so do I. It just seems all so serendipitous that I feel like I'm inside a dream. I don't think this is how the day of my husband's memorial service is supposed to end."

He smiled. "We never have come together under the most conventional of circumstances."

"True enough. I'm afraid that when you walk away from me tonight, you'll change your mind. You'll go back to your life, and I'll go back to mine. Then what happens?"

"Whatever we make happen."

She closed her eyes and exhaled slowly.

"Temira, are you ready for this? You need to allow yourself time to grieve."

She opened her eyes and looked into his. "I threw away a chance with you once. I'm not doing it again. You want this, right?"

"I wasn't trying to get out of it. I just want to make sure you're ready."

"Why don't you let me decide when I'm ready?" Her tone sounded more defensive than she intended.

Silence settled between them for a minute.

"Of course, Temira. I just meant I don't want you to feel pressured or rushed. I don't want to be your rebound relationship."

She smiled. "Isn't every relationship after the first relationship a rebound relationship to some degree? I understand your point, Burke. Truly I do, and I don't want to hurt you. I know the dangers of rushing into a relationship while grieving."

"Okay, then we'll take things slowly. Let this relationship build as we get to know one another again."

She nodded.

He hugged her and turned to leave. He stopped and looked back.

"So, Temira, what are you going to do now?"

"Take a chance."

Coming Soon

Red (A Novel)

Chapter 1

Tears streamed down Marissa's cheeks, her long light brown hair fell over her face and stuck to her cheeks. Marissa sat in the middle of her kitchen surrounded by those she loved – the only three people in the world who mattered to her. She stared at them, clueless as to what she should do next.

The sun streaking the sky with oranges, pinks, and purples interrupted by gray rolling clouds, the wind blowing through the trees in the backyard, and the distant sounds of thunder signaling an approaching storm felt like a different reality. One in which she had no place. The evening storm moved toward the house, finally cooling the sun's rays which had punished anyone who dared step outdoors all day. She barely heard the thunder crash – louder, closer. The red in front of her blocked out everything else as it consumed her.

She ran her index finder through the sea of red covering the white ceramic tile floor. Her eyes refused to look up. If she didn't see the source of the red maybe, just maybe, she could convince herself it was only paint. Paint. Yeah, that was it. Paint. Red paint. Lots of red paint. She whispered the word aloud, or did she? "Paint."

It didn't surround those she loved so dearly. It couldn't. They didn't deserve the red. The flood of red came after her like it had so many times before. Why wouldn't it stop?

Her ivory pants darkened as the red spread over them. She watched it but couldn't force herself to move away from the sensation of wetness against her knees. She should move. She needed to call for help, but she couldn't move, couldn't speak, couldn't breathe. Her mind froze and her body paralyzed in place.

Her loved ones came into focus as she lifted her head. They lay next to each other on the floor. The red oozed from their bodies blending with the red surrounding her. She shook her head. Streaks of blood created paths from her to them. She looked to her side and picked up the bloodstained 8-inch serrated bread knife. She would join her family. Yes, that's what she'd do. It was the only answer. Two bloody bread crumbs dropped from the knife and landed on her upper thigh. She leaned forward. She felt the red dye her ivory camisole and her forehead. Red never stayed where it belonged. Her hand wound around the blade. The cold, hard steel cut through the skin on her palm, but she felt little more than a tingling sensation. She closed her eyes. The fight left her. The red could have her.

The tip of the knife cut through her paints and separated the skin on her leg. She continued the slow, precise movement without so much as a change of expression. Blood seeped from the wound in her leg and the gash in her hand.

A sudden, large crash of thunder and a flash of lightning interrupted the ominous quiet. The rain had yet to come. Marissa shuddered still focused on the encroaching red. This time her defenses were gone. It would take her like it had threatened so many times before.

Minutes passed.

She sat up and stared at the motionless bodies spread in a neat row in the entrance from the family room to the kitchen. The knife dropped from her hand with a clang as metal hit ceramic. She twitched her nose against the assault of a coppery odor. Her gaze traveled from one lifeless body to the next. From the small, pretty girl to the even smaller cute boy to the handsome man. They shared enough features to prove they were related. Who were these people? Why am I sitting in this room with them? Where am I? Do they mean something to me? Should they mean something to me? How did they get here? How did I get here?

Marissa turned her head toward a rustling noise in the backyard. Her green eyes met the red-rimmed, tear filled, green eyes of a stranger in her reflection in the sliding glass doors. She shuddered as the thought of evil lurking nearby washed over her. She pushed her hair away from her face. The door stood slightly open and the wind whipped through the space, whistling a barely audible whine. Or was that sound stuck in her throat trying to get out?

Well-known sounds in the next room attracted her attention. She looked around to find the source of the sounds. Tom chased Jerry on the television. Between her and the television lay those familiar, lifeless bodies surrounded by a sea of rising red. Her body shook violently as she struggled to bring the bodies into face, to remember what she needed to remember, to understand what stood just beyond her comprehension.

She clutched her head in her hands. Who the hell were these people? She needed to remember. She knew they were important. It was important she remember them. She pulled her hair How did the red find them? How had they gotten here? What had happened to them? She beat her bloody hands against her blood-covered face. Thoughts, so many thoughts, kept swirling in her head. They made no sense. Faces and red and people and red and places and red. Always the red. She couldn't stop the red. Too much red.

Rain beat against the sliding glass door and the kitchen window matching the banging inside her head. Marissa continued to beat her hands against her face but otherwise remained still.

She heard sirens in the distance. Help was on the way....

Red is scheduled for release in late 2018!

T. L. Cooper

The Gratitude Gift:
Lessons in Love, Life, & Loss

Chapter 1

When I decided to focus on gratitude for an entire year, I had no idea where it would go. It seemed so simple. I would meditate on gratitude, post something I felt grateful for – unique each day – on Facebook, and continue to write in my gratitude journal each night.

Simple enough.

And it was simple in some ways.

I loved it. I loved thinking about the good in my life. I loved seeing the abundance in my life. I loved seeing people through new eyes. I loved seeing experiences through a positive filter rather than a victimization filter. It felt awesome.

Then...

There's always a then.

I started seeing areas in my life that weren't working. I couldn't hide from certain realities anymore. Focusing on gratitude somehow lead me to the place of seeing there were problems I'd been ignoring in order to avoid conflict and not have to do the hard work. I saw, for the first time in a long time, all the masks I'd been hiding behind, trying desperately to be perfect, to be loveable.

Gratitude freed me from my need to be perfect and left me feeling a bit rudderless while at the same time I felt more connected to life than I'd imagined possible. In the midst of all this, my marriage hit one of its rockiest points ever. I was sure we were headed for divorce.

And yet, I didn't feel as devastated as the few friends I confided in thought I should. Each day I continued to focus on gratitude even when, perhaps especially when, it felt like gratitude was a luxury I didn't deserve. Yet, I found comfort in searching for gratitude on a daily basis, even on the days when it felt like I needed a magical spell to conjure it.

People on Facebook began to tell me how much my daily

gratitude posts meant to them. I felt strange about that because I had days when the posts felt more like obligations even though the meditations always helped me find my bearings and gave me hope.

So how did I meditate on gratitude? It was really a formal process. There's no deep, life-changing secret to the process. I simply sat down and thought. First I thought about gratitude in the abstract. Then I focused in on people, events, moments, emotions, words, even memories that I felt grateful for. Most days this took less than five minutes, but some days it's took fifteen or twenty minutes. Choosing something to post often took longer than tuning into gratitude. Releasing my concerns about people's reactions was harder than finding gratitude. I would fret about the wording or someone misinterpreting my intention. I would often draft several versions before choosing one to post.

Along the way, I rediscovered my inner strength and vulnerability. I also concluded that my strength often makes me feel vulnerable, but I also feel stronger when I tap into my vulnerability. The interwoven nature of strength and vulnerability surprised me and continues to play a huge role in my life, my work, my interactions with both myself and others.

Gratitude pushed me to seek out the things in life that truly brought me pleasure, joy, and fulfillment while also encouraging me to let go of the things that drained me energetically, physically, mentally, and emotionally.

Every aspect of my life improved as I journeyed through 2011 seeking gratitude and building on the positive in my life. Part of that improvement came by way of acknowledging not only the good in my life but the bad. To maintain gratitude I had to deal with the bad instead of ignoring it. To do otherwise was disingenuous.

A friend once asked me if focusing so much on gratitude made me feel like a "Pollyanna". I can sincerely say that it didn't. In fact, focusing on gratitude ended up having the opposite effect on me and my life. It forced me to stop trying to project a positive image and tune in to my real feelings for better or worse.

It also forced me to see my flaws. I confronted my insecurities, my tendency toward jealousy, my fear of abandonment, the secret pain I couldn't release, my fear of being found, and even what love meant to me. Through the experiment I confronted my past, my present, and what I wanted for the future.

Gratitude in that it opened doors and windows I thought I'd long closed, locked, and boarded up. My simple experiment to use gratitude to become more positive about my life turned into a complex examination of my life, my relationships, and my self.

The Gratitude Gift is scheduled for release in 2018!

Book List

Fiction

All She Ever Wanted

Soaring Betrayal (short stories)

Poetry

Love in Silhouette: Poems

Reflections in Silhouette: Poems

Memory in Silhouette: Poems

Strength in Silhouette: Poems

Vulnerability in Silhouette: Poems

Praise for T. L. Cooper's Books

Soaring Betrayal

"…leaves one feeling as if the reader's and the writer's hearts and souls are speaking to each other.…" – Anthony V. Toscano

Strength in Silhouette

"…Often harsh in its realism, it also can soar with delicate and unexpected nuance…" - Lucy

Memory in Silhouette

"…pithy examination of relational memories should help every poet discover an inner part of their own memories. I highly recommend this poetic study in life lived and memories examined." – Auburn McCanta, author of All the Dancing Birds

Reflections in Silhouette

"…Brave enough to lower the curtain into her own heart, T.L. gives the reader that certain leverage where one might be able to find the strength, upon reflection, to go forward into the bright sunshine of their own new day…" - Ray Ellis, author of the Nate Richards Series.

Love in Silhouette

"…Love in Silhouette" is a delightfully honest and open-faced collection of poetry that leaves you feeling as though you have peeked in on intimate moments of the author's love life…" - Mary Braun, co-author of Opposites Attract: A Haiku Tete-a-Tete.

All She Ever Wanted

"…A thoughtful, insightful look into the changing human mind and spirit evoked by an interracial friendship, All She Ever Wanted is a superbly written, highly recommended novel showcasing a theme that is as historic and universal as interracial human experience, and contemporary as today's newspaper headlines…" - Midwest Book Review.

About the Author

T. L. Cooper is an author and poet whose work aims to empower and inspire through an exploration of the human condition. Her poems, short stories, articles, and essays have appeared online, in books, and in magazines. Her published books include a collection of short stories, *Soaring Betrayal*, her *Silhouette Poetry Series*, and a novel, *All She Ever Wanted*. She grew up on a farm in Tollesboro, Kentucky. When not writing, she enjoys yoga, golf, hiking, and traveling. She currently lives in Albany, Oregon with her husband and three cats.